Marshall, William   Mystery
Perfect end

8/83

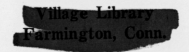

PERFECT END

A RINEHART SUSPENSE NOVEL

Other Yellowthread Street Mysteries

YELLOWTHREAD STREET
THE HATCHET MAN
GELIGNITE
THIN AIR
SKULDUGGERY
SCI FI

Also by William Marshall

SHANGHAI

A RINEHART SUSPENSE NOVEL

PERFECT END

A YELLOWTHREAD STREET MYSTERY

William Marshall

HOLT, RINEHART AND WINSTON
New York

MYSTERY

Library of Congress Cataloging in Publication Data
Marshall, William Leonard, 1944–
Perfect end.
I. Title.
PR9619.3.M275P4 1983   823   82-15502
ISBN 0-03-047481-7

First American Edition
Printed in the United States of America
10 9 8 7 6 5 4 3 2 1

ISBN 0-03-047481-7

The Hong Bay district of Hong Kong
is fictitious, as are the people who,
for one reason or another, inhabit it.

Cats and Dogs

In Fade Street at 7.55 in the morning, The Umbrella Man was a portrait of dejected, pathetic misery. Not that anyone could *see* The Umbrella Man to characterise him as the last repository of Chinese woe and total, abject commercial failure – oh, no, that would have been too much to ask.

In Fade Street only the rain was having a good time and The Umbrella Man, fixing a bitter smile to his face, nodded at the sleeting, pouring, driving water ruining his stock, his clientele, and his family's future and thought venomously, 'I'm glad for you. I'm glad you're having a good time. I'm glad you're not just a light drizzle the way the Weather Bureau said you would be' – a cascade of water crashed through a tear in a beach umbrella protecting his makeshift stall and ruined all his stock – 'I'm *delighted you're a stinking goddamned flood!*'

And the dog. Across the street, the dog in the goddamned Fade Street police station had kept up an uninterrupted, non-stop top-volume howling for the last two hours. The Umbrella Man said between clenched teeth, 'I'm going to kill that dog. So help me, if it's the last thing I do before hunger and bankruptcy send me straight into the nearest charity lazar house to gasp out my few remaining moments, I'm going to go across to the police station, grab that dog by the throat – and then I'm going to throttle the life out of it!'

The rain paused for a moment and, in the customerless street, The Umbrella Man, fearing that he might have said something to offend it in its sworn task of drowning him, his business, and the entire Colony of Hong Kong under an ocean of cloud piss, threw three of his umbrellas on the ground, stamped on them, and shrieked at it at the top of his voice, 'No, don't stop! You're doing fine! You've almost ruined me! Don't stop! If you stop, a customer might venture out into the weather and buy a goddamned *umbrella!*'

The rain, no doubt the advance guard of nothing less than a catastrophic, planet-tilting typhoon building up somewhere out in the South China Sea, paused, hissing, to think that one over.

The Umbrella Man railed, 'Don't think it over! I've invested my entire life's savings on umbrellas and I've still got a few left you haven't saturated! Don't stop now or you might leave me just a little hope that maybe I could go on living in the poorhouse or in an alley somewhere in reduced circumstances!' The dog released a howl from somewhere in the police station of nothing less than elephantine proportions. The Umbrella Man yelled, 'Listen to your friend the dog – you know, the soul in torment that even if you weren't pissing down on them would scare the shit out of any potential customer who might accidentally happen this way – don't give up now: do a good job and drown me where I stand!' The rain, shifting direction slightly from sweeping down the centre of the street, poured onto him like a waterfall. The Umbrella Man said, 'I'm going to kill that dog! So help me, if I go to prison for it for a thousand years, so help me I'm going to kill that dog!'

The dog, reaching new heights of dementia, must have laid back its head, pointed its muzzle in the general direction of The Umbrella Man, and let fly. A moan of terrible throbbing volume rose up and echoed in the grey

2

vault of the sky. The Umbrella Man found his best quality, most expensive indestructible handmade in a sweat shop umbrella, ripped the spokes and fabric from it, jabbed its point into his overhead parasol to test its rapier qualities, and, advancing in the direction of the station, said conversationally to the rain, 'I'll be back in a moment. I'm just going across the road to the cop shop to skewer that dog to the heart. I'll probably be unsuccessful because no doubt the dog belongs to one of the cops who thinks that noise is nothing less than the authentic music of Paradise and when I try to kill it he'll beat me into a bloody pulp, but I don't mind, why should I mind? In my own way, I'm happy.'

The Umbrella Man, his future as a pauper decided for once and for all and all those nagging aspirations and doubts of a lifetime of worry finally and irretrievably disposed of, went across the street, stood looking up at the sky so the rain could have a last solid go at him before he entered criminal incarceration forever, and pushed the front door of the station open.

The front door of the station didn't push open.

A torrent of rain, evidently having been building itself up on the roof for this very moment, fell down like a blanket and saturated him.

The dog went on howling.

The Umbrella Man, shrugging, said, 'Great. Obviously, the cop who owns the dog knows I'm coming and when he shoots me dead for carrying a deadly weapon he wants to do it around the back where the blood won't stain the carpet in the front office.' The Umbrella Man said, 'I can understand that. When I was alive I had carpets and mats and things too.' The Umbrella Man called out at the locked door, 'Fine, fine! Anything to oblige. I'll go around to the back.' The Umbrella Man, making his way through the – of course – three inch deep river of water pouring down the driveway of the rear carpark of the station, glanced inside one of the warm, dry police cars parked there. Before he had sunk to the level of irredeemable bumhood, he had thought about owning a car too. The dog and the rain had fixed that.

The Umbrella Man tested the point of his umbrella. The dog, telepathically forewarned, stopped its howling for a moment, and The Umbrella Man, sloshing through the slough of despond by yet another parked rich people type automobile, shouted, 'Don't stop, you mangy scumbags soon-to-be-spitted god-forgotten hound – *keep howling*!' reached the corner of the building, tensed himself for the shoulder on the door, the quick charge down the length of the station corridor, the yell of conquest as he sighted the slavering enemy, the heady, blood-letting surge of triumph as the great fang dripping beast felt cold steel in its—

The Umbrella Man looked at a sudden picture of small, dejected pathetic misery tied to the back door of the police station and said, 'Oh.' A pair of mournful brown eyes gazed sadly at him from a slightly cocked, sodden head. A single tear glistened in a downcast canine eye. A —

The Umbrella Man said again, 'Oh...'

The dog, hoping, wagged its tail...

The Umbrella Man put down his umbrella.

The brown eyes looked at him...

The Umbrella Man said softly...

The rain, taking absolutely no notice of this touching scene at all, continued to piss down with unabated frenzy and The Umbrella Man shouted, 'Fucking rain! You spoil everything, don't you!'

For a moment, The Umbrella Man saw a shadow at one of the darkened windows at the side of the building. It was a trick of the light. The Umbrella Man bent down to the dog and untied it and patted it on the head. The Umbrella Man said to the dog, 'Come on, we'll get you inside.' The shadow was gone. He pushed open the rear door of the police station and saw what looked like claw marks on the plaster wall of the empty lobby. The Umbrella Man, still patting the dog, went through the lobby and into the squadroom.

There were coffee cups on the desks in there, and papers arranged in the trays and lying piled up on blotters. An open fountain pen lay by one of the piles and, to the left of it, a bottle of black ink with the unscrewed cap lying beside it. There was a revolver on a side table next to a cleaning kit, the six brass cartridges standing next to it like a little row of lead-helmeted soldiers. There was a wall clock by the rear door to the room ticking away loudly. The Umbrella Man said cautiously, 'Hullo—? Is anyone here?'

A phone was ringing in another room somewhere. The Umbrella Man went out the rear door into a long corridor and saw more scratches on the wall. The Umbrella Man said again, 'Hullo? I've found—'

The rain was easing on the tiled roof above his head. The Umbrella Man could still hear the wall clock in the room behind him. He went into the charge room and saw a police overcoat hung neatly on a coat hanger on a hat rack.

The phone, wherever it was, stopped ringing, and the station was silent.

The dog made a sudden low growling noise and stopped.

The Umbrella Man said nervously, 'Hullo. Um. Is anyone—?' He saw another deep claw mark on a wall. The claw mark seemed to have been made by a single sharp talon. The mark ground its way down the plaster from about chest height and then, unaccountably, stopped. The Umbrella Man heard the dog behind him make a noise in its throat.

The room where The Umbrella Man thought he had seen a shadow in the carpark was behind a closed door in front of him. Even the sound of the rain seemed to have stopped. On the charge room desk there was another cup of coffee, half drunk. The Umbrella Man touched the cup. It was cold. He looked at the ashtray near the cup. There was

5

a single cigarette in it that had burned all the way down into ash without anyone picking it up to smoke it.

The Umbrella Man looked down at the dog and saw it was shivering.

The Umbrella Man, his mouth dry, said softly in the direction of the closed door in front of him, 'Hullo? Is there anyone there?'

He looked down at the floor. It had been raining all night, but apart from his own tracks and those of the dog, there was not the faintest mark on it. It had been polished recently. He could smell the wax. The Umbrella Man said, nervously, as the door in front of him began to open slowly, 'Um, it's about the – it's about the dog...' In that room, as the door opened – where he had seen the shadow – there was pitch darkness.

The Umbrella Man said, 'All the—!'

Facing him in the half light of the charge room, looking out at him with wide unblinking staring, monstrous eyes, was the head of a single, giant cat, standing, like a man, erect.

The Umbrella Man, his mouth fallen open, said, 'All the—'

The cat had a silver butterfly in its mouth and it appeared, before it had been disturbed and had had to turn the knob and open the door of the darkened room, to be in the process of putting the butterfly in its mouth.

The butterfly, still alive, fluttered for an instant.

The butterfly had three wings.

The Umbrella Man said, *'All the gods in Heaven*!!' and, a moment before he and the dog fled from the empty station with the rain again falling heavily down on the roof above them, the door to the darkened room closed again and the cat was gone.

The station was full of claw marks.

The Umbrella Man saw more of them as he ran.

*

In the darkened room, a moment after the door closed and the lock snicked back into place, there was a single note.

The Umbrella Man heard it. A note... It sounded for all the world like someone plucking a single note on a slightly out of tune bass cello.

Then the sound was gone and in the Fade Street police station between the neighbouring precincts of Hong Bay and North Point at 8.21 a.m., as the rain ceased for the third time that morning, there was an utter, still, sepulchral silence.

1

There weren't no rain that never bothered no backwoods mountain-man, no cloud spit that never counted for no sassy-panced high buttoned boot in hell when it came to bein' grizzled. No spittoon in Sassafras county that never ... At the rain running window of the Detectives' Room in the Yellowthread Street police station, Hong Bay, Detective Senior Inspector Christopher O'Yee shaving himself with a knife the size of an Arkansas tooth-pick, said, 'Ouch! *That hurt!*'

Across from him, watching from his desk with a pained expression of sympathy and lunatic-humouring, Detective Chief Inspector Harry Feiffer said, 'Are you all right? Why don't you use the electric razor in the—'

'Because backwoodsmen don't have electric razors for the simple reason they don't have electric sockets to plug them into.' O'Yee raised the giant blade again, 'It's not my bloody fault if I happened to inherit my father's Chinese skin. If I'd inherited more from my Irish mother I'd have bigger whiskers to shave.'

Feiffer said, 'Right.' He watched in awful fascination as the silver blade went scrape, scrape, scrape across O'Yee's cheek, 'Any chance that the true backwoodsman might prefer to grow a beard?'

O'Yee gave him a snorting noise. (Feiffer had an awful feeling that if he spoke too loudly while the terrible operation was progressing that the snorting noise might terminate in a jugular-bleeding noise.) O'Yee said, 'I happen to be American by birth and I've reached middle age and like all true-born Americans of middle age I feel the great oudoors calling to me.' He turned to face Feiffer with a careless swoop of the knife that put Feiffer's heart into his mouth, 'I intend to shave every day just like this to toughen myself up so I can survive in the wild.' O'Yee said, still waving the knife, 'I've had enough of this cop business. The time has come in my life to make a move and I intend to move back to the Great Outdoors and the savage nature of my primitive forefathers.'

Feiffer, smiling, one eye still on the ghastly knife, said, 'Oh. Good.' Anything to keep him talking, 'I suppose this decision is irrevocable, is it?'

'It is, yes.' O'Yee said, 'You won't understand this, Harry, being born in Hong Kong, but there is in every American soul a yearning to be free and at one with nature. You won't have read *The Red Badge Of Courage*. (Feiffer said, 'I have actually.' He was ignored.) But like The Youth, in all of us there is a need to face The Great Death in the loneliness of the vast—'

Feiffer said, 'You will write?' He could see O'Yee working himself up to a bit of face paring to emphasise his point, 'I mean, I'd like to know how it goes, or, um – or send you salt pork or something...'

'Letters take a long time by paddle steamer.'

'I didn't think they still had them.' He saw immediately from O'Yee's face that it had been meant as some sort of deep, good earth proverb. Feiffer said, 'Oh, I see. Right. Of course they do.' He gave O'Yee an apologetic smile, 'I must admit I didn't read that one.' Feiffer said, 'What else does a backwoodsman do?' He hoped as he pondered it, O'Yee wouldn't rest the point of the knife pensively against the thin flesh of his chin.

O'Yee rested the knife pensively against the thick pine of his desk. O'Yee said, 'He learns to shoot straight.'

'You can do that already.'

'—with his muzzle loader.'

Feiffer said helpfully, 'Easy really—'

'And he toughens himself up.'

'No trouble for a fit individual like you.' Feiffer tried to remember what he had heard middle-aged American executives greet each other with in the local Hilton hotel before a meal so full of fats and cholesterol it would have killed a cow. Feiffer said, 'Sonofabitch, you look hard gutted to me.' With an English accent it just didn't sound right. Feiffer said, 'I'm sure Emily looks after you all right.'

The knife waved that part of his past life away. 'Emily's days of looking after me are over. All Emily has to do is keep the log fire burning until her man packs home the dead deer meat.' O'Yee said, 'Rat meat, that's what the old pioneers lived on in the winters, raw meat and the leather from their boots.'

Feiffer said, 'Really?' He saw a suspicious glint form in the old timer's eye that told him at a glance that when an Easterner said, 'Really?' to an old timer in a voice that carried even the faintest suspicion of city-slicker smart-assing then the smart-assed city slicker had better start watching his ass. Feiffer said, 'Of course, you know in those days they used mules to get about.'

'They used feet!' O'Yee said, 'All this Walt Disney stuff is crap. Those old guys didn't have mules to get about on because in winter they ate their mules. They walked, and that's what I intend to do.'

Feiffer said, 'Right. As soon as it stops raining you can walk over to Fade Street and see what's keeping Auden and Spencer—'

'They walked in the rain. In the rain those old guys worked up a walking sweat so hot the rain just turned into mist around them and the sun came straight through the

10

holes in the clouds.' O'Yee said, 'I've been reading in this book that not one of those old guys died of heart attacks or cancer or strokes or—'

Feiffer said mildly, 'What did they die of?'

O'Yee said quietly, 'Fear.' He looked at the wet window for a long moment and in the reflection Feiffer could see there were tears in his eyes. O'Yee said very quietly, 'They woke up in the middle of the night listening to their hearts beating away and counting their birthdays and they died of fear, Harry.' He looked down at the huge knife in his hand and put it gently on the window sill, 'Just like I'm going to.' He said quickly, 'Those old back-woodsmen, when the hell did you ever see them look worried?'

Feiffer, getting up from his desk, said gently, 'Hey, Christopher...'

O'Yee said brightly, 'Yeah, I'll live to be a hundred.'

'Sure.' Feiffer said lightly, 'Who the hell ever heard of a Chinese backwoodsman anyway?'

Goddamit, that was the exact same thing his wife has said! O'Yee said fiercely, 'I did! What about Pine Cone Pin?' He picked up the giant knife again.

Feiffer said, 'Oh, him! I'd overlooked him completely!'

He had forgotten to watch his ass. The grizzled old timer, his soul in tune with rat meat and shoe leather, saw through him with a single withering stare, and, silently, intensely, began shaving in the reflection of the window again.

*

The interior of the car was filling up with cigarette smoke. Blue and acrid, it hung about against the grey, rain washed windscreen. The occupant of the car wound down his side window a fraction and it escaped in whisps into the rain of Fade Street and was replaced by the warm smell of the rain. The driver was sweating: he wiped at his forehead with his knuckles, looked across towards the driveway of the police station as The Umbrella Man in the back of the Yellowthread Street car parked there turned at the rear window to show the dog something across the road.

It was the lost mongrel someone had brought into the station the night before last. In his smoke filled car Staff Sergeant Shen of Fade Street ducked his head as The Umbrella Man pointed the dog's head in what looked like his direction and gave the sodden little mutt a pat.

Sergeant Shen's service revolver was on the seat next to him, its white lanyard unclipped from its belt and lying loose on the floor.

He saw movement at the back of the station – two detectives from Yellowthread Street – Auden and... The other one moved out of sight behind a car and he couldn't identify him. Shen ran his tongue across his lips and touched at the butt of his gun.

The Umbrella Man and his cursed dog turned away from the rear window of the car for a moment and Shen turned on his ignition and, afraid to put on the windscreen wipers in case someone noticed him, drove very slowly and carefully down the deserted street and made the turn into Singapore Road, leaning forward almost against his running windscreen like some sort of nervous learner driver anxious to gain as much proximity as possible between him and the hostile road.

Once around the turn, he switched on the wipers and, his hands abruptly trembling on the wheel, holding in a silent scream, he jammed his foot down hard on the gas pedal and, the tyres spinning in protest on the wet road, accelerated away from that awful place into the suddenly welcoming concealment of the rain.

*

In Fade Street, Detective Inspector Auden said with a snarl, 'This had better not be somebody's idea of a joke, I'm telling you.' Like Detective Inspector Spencer, he was padding carefully along the waxed corridor in his socks holding his trouser legs up like a crinolined lady bather so he wouldn't make marks on the floor. Auden said warningly, 'If some cop suddenly jumps out of one of these rooms with a camera and thinks he's got the greatest stupid cop picture since the shooting of Lee Harvey Oswald then he's going to be wearing his flashbulb in his tonsils!' There was another claw mark on the wall. Auden said, 'Another one.' Spencer was walking carefully in his faint footprints. Auden said, 'Mind where you walk.' He came to the squadroom and saw the open bottle of ink and the fountain pen ready for refilling. Rain was beating heavily on the roof. Auden said, pausing, 'You don't get big cats in Hong Kong do you, Bill?'

Spencer said, 'The lights are on.' He gazed around the deserted room and saw a coffee cup with the coffee in it making a caked stain half way down. Spencer said quietly, 'Phil, when you've come in from a job where do you put your gun?' He went over carefully across the heavily waxed floor and pulled open the top drawer in the nearest desk with his finger.

Auden said, 'In the top drawer of my desk.' There was a holstered revolver in the top drawer of the desk and, next to it, a pair of stainless steel handcuffs. Auden said, 'Hell—!' There was a single claw mark against the back of the wooden chair at the desk: a deep, ripping indentation that seemed to half swirl then stop. Auden leaned down and sniffed at it. The back of the chair too had been waxed. There was the faintest odour of disinfectant about it. The lights dimmed momentarily with a flash of lightning outside and Auden said unnecessarily, 'The chair's been cleaned too.'

Spencer said, 'Hullo, is there anybody here—?'

13

Auden asked softly, 'Do you know any of these people? Any of the cops?'

Spencer shook his head.

Auden touched at the butt of his gun under his coat. 'They're not musical any of them, are they?'

Spencer looked at him curiously.

'I mean, the cello note or whatever it was The Umbrella Man—' There was a creaking sound from the ceiling and Auden's hand tightened around his gun. It was the rain pattering down on the tiled roof. Auden said, 'It's like some sort of museum.' He said suddenly, 'You locked that bugger in, did you? The Umbrella Man – in the back of the car?'

Spencer nodded. Carefully, he put his hand on the seat of the chair and felt it. It was cold. Spencer said a long time after Auden had asked the question, 'Yes, he can't get out.' He peered over at something on the floor and then silently indicated it with his finger – a little lump of floor wax still showing the swirls from an electric waxing machine. There was an odd smell in the room blended in with the wax, like death. Spencer said, 'It's as if they suddenly—' He turned quickly as Auden's voice said from the door of the room, 'Another mark.' He was looking across to where the disassembled gun lay on a table with the cleaning kit spread out around it. There was a scuffled series of footprints around it – The Umbrella Man. Auden said, 'We'd better go into the charge room.'

Pausing, Spencer said, 'There is some sort of rare giant cat in Hong Kong. It's called a Chinese leopard cat but it's very rare, and it doesn't—' He followed Auden into the charge room and saw the closed door behind which the cat – Chinese leopard or otherwise – had been seen. There was another claw mark on the wall of the charge room, ripped into the plaster of the wall, long and jagged, terminating a foot from the floor. The floor of the charge

14

room had also been waxed. He looked across at the front door of the station. It had been bolted from inside.

The charge room, like everything else in the station, was deserted. There were only the footprints where The Umbrella Man had walked. His prints were over the wax. Spencer said softly, 'If whatever it is isn't in that room then there's only the old air raid shelter left.' He jerked his head at the closed door. 'This place was built at about the same time as Yellowthread Street. When I was in Administration I remember looking through some of the old plans from the War when they—' Auden was looking at the closed door. Under his coat, his hand was around the butt of his long barreled Colt Python. There was a non-regulation .357 magnum round in one of the chambers of the otherwise regulation loaded .38 Special weapon. With his eyes still on the door, Auden snapped open the cylinder of the gun and turned the magnum round so that it was first in line. Auden said nervously, 'If there's a bloody cat in there—' He turned to Spencer and shrugged. Auden said very quietly, 'I don't care much for bloody ghost stories...'He took a step forward and then turned again to look at Spencer.

There was a total of six claw marks, at least one in every room of the station. The lights dimmed for a moment and Spencer could hear the rain beating insistently on the roof. Spencer said, swallowing, 'It's some sort of storeroom, I think, or—' To one side of the door there was a plastic light switch. It was set to the off position.

Auden said, 'Turn it on.'

Spencer's hand paused above the butt of his own revolver in its leather belt holster. Spencer said dubiously, 'We can't just ... I mean, what if it's some sort of joke, or—'

Auden said, 'Turn it on.'

'But if it's—' Spencer said quickly, 'All right.' He went forward and snapped the switch down. Through the crack

15

in the door above the floor, no light appeared. He listened.

Nothing.

For a moment, the light dimmed in the charge room.

The rain was pattering on the roof. Like some sort of deserted haunted house, dust was settling slowly onto the floor. There was no sound from behind the closed door.

The claw marks were everywhere in the station, ripped deeply into walls and chairs and then, washed over and waxed.

And coffee cups, half finished, a gun lying open to be cleaned, cigarettes burned down in—

Auden, with his breath coming fast and hard, the huge gun gripped firmly ahead of him in the classic combat-ready hold, said, 'Fuck it, Bill, whatever is in that goddamned room, I swear to you – is fucking ... *dead*!'

He put his shoulder suddenly to the door, broke it down with a tearing, protesting splintering of wood and wrenching metal and, with Spencer only a second behind him with his own gun out, disappeared in there into the darkness.

There was a flash of lightning in the sky outside that blew out the fuses with a staccato crack and all the lights in the station went out.

*

In the Detectives' Room at Yellowthread Street, Feiffer held the receiver of his telephone out for O'Yee to hear.

The phone was working and the ringing burr from the other end of the line went on and on and on. Feiffer said, 'That's odd. That's the general number for the entire place so even if there isn't anyone in the squadroom some-one in the charge room should hear it.' He paused for a moment with a thought reluctantly forming, 'Even if there isn't anyone else there, then Auden or Spencer—' He replaced the receiver and, checking the Fade

Street number in the police directory as O'Yee riffled through the pages of the general Hong Kong phone book, asked, 'What number have you got for them there?'

O'Yee read it out. It was the same.

It was the third time in the last half hour that Feiffer had tried to ring. He rang Central Despatch and asked them for the second time whether the atmospherics had cleared and they could raise Auden and Spencer on the car radio.

With the rain and the lightning, Fade Street had become a dead spot on the network.

With a worried expression starting on his face, Feiffer lit a cigarette and, dialling very slowly and carefully to make sure he had all the digits absolutely correct, rang Fade Street yet again.

*

In the Weather Bureau, the satellite pictures made any further guesswork unnecessary. It was a typhoon and it was building up about three hundred and fifty miles out to sea. The rainstorms were its precursors. Wandering, the typhoon was presently heading in a north easterly direction, its far swirling arms seeming to break away as if it was trying to pull the epicentre of the cataclysm away towards the Taiwan Strait and the Japanese Ryukyu Islands.

The epicentre of the hurricane, however, showed no signs of being pulled anywhere. Seething as a white spinning out of control wheel, growing fast on the satellite pictures, it was heading due north, moving fast.

The Thunderstorm And Heavy Rain Warning Service, at an alert signal from the Bureau, swung smoothly into routine action, and as part of that routine made contact with police stations all over the Colony to warn them that

17

Warning Signal One was in operation and that they were to stand by.

The only station not replying was Fade Street, but the system – a series of telephone calls from the Post Office telephone centre – was staffed by human beings and, unlike machines, they simply assumed that if they couldn't contact them now they would simply contact them later.

So far this year there had been almost the full quota of typhoons and, having last utilised Olga as the great winds' sobriquet, the staff at the Weather Bureau set about thinking up a brand new name for their latest meteorological visitor.

One of the forecasters at the Bureau had had a vaguely classical education before going into Science at university and he thought he had the ideal moniker for what looked like being the typhoon of the year.

*

Feiffer's phone rang. Auden said, 'Harry, we've found them. Bill's with them now in the old air raid shelter in the basement. We broke into the room where the cat was supposed to be and we've had flashlights in there, and we—' His voice sounded very odd. 'And they're all dead. They're in the old air raid shelter in a row, all in full uniform, the whole lot of them, laid out like wine bottles in a—' He said again, 'They're all dead. Cops, just like you and me and—' He drew a breath. 'You'd better get over here. Bill's with them now and—' There was a long pause. Auden said with his voice breaking, 'My God, Harry, it's like something out of some sort of bloody horror movie – the whole place is like – ' There was a burst of interference on the line and then Auden's voice said, horror-struck at the sudden realisation, 'We even found a claw mark in one of the toilets, on the back wall – what-

18

ever, whoever killed one of them in there even – must have even pulled the poor bastard's trousers up before he – ' Auden's voice said on the edge of hysteria, '*Harry, the whole place has been cleaned and waxed and polished like some sort of bloody Egyptian pyramid, like it was done by some sort of, of—*'

Auden said, 'It's all these goddamned claw marks – I just don't know *what the hell made them!*'

Through the receiver, Feiffer actually heard the crack as, above Fade Street, lightning lit up the sky and all the lights in the station came on again together.

*

Hong Kong is an island of 30 square miles under British administration in the South China Sea facing Kowloon and the New Territories area of continental China. Kowloon and the New Territories are also British administered, surrounded by the Communist Chinese province of Kwantung. The climate is generally sub-tropical, with hot, humid summers, cold winters, and heavy rainfall. The population of Hong Kong and the surrounding areas at any one time is in excess of four and a half millions. The New Territories are leased from the Chinese. The lease is due to expire in 1997, but the British nevertheless maintain a military presence along the border, although should the Communists, who supply almost all the Colony's drinking water, ever desire to terminate the lease early, they need only turn off the taps. Hong Bay is on the southern side of the island and the tourist brochures advise you not to go there after dark.

*

The Weather Bureau, at the forecaster's request, approved the name for the typhoon.

The north easterly arm of the disturbance had been pulled back into the centre of the boiling mass and its

19

direction was in an almost straight line towards Hong Kong.

Pandora.

Not usually noted for it, the men at the Weather Bureau thought it at least showed a sense of ironic humour.

2

In the dim half light of the shielded safety lights of the air raid shelter the scene looked like something from the Borgias' cellars after the Christmas poisonings. Squatting down in his long black apron on the bare stone floor, Doctor Macarthur inserted a long glittering stainless steel probe into the chest wound in the uniformed European Superintendent lying at the head of the row, pushed it through with a lack of hesitation that made Spencer wince and, expelling a long breath, knelt closer to the body and peered into the bloody hole with a pencil flashlight like Philip Marlowe after secrets at a keyhole. The other five bodies, all uniformed Chinese Constables, lay in the same attitude as the Superintendent, their arms straight by their sides as if at attention, and Macarthur, completing his torchlight examination, glanced at them briefly as a group, then, narrowing his eyes, shook his head.

Spencer, kneeling beside him, moved to a squatting position and for something to do, looked down to his pants knees to brush them. The air raid shelter was spotlessly clean and his knees were not dusty. Upstairs, he could hear Feiffer and Auden treading lightly on the floorboards then a pause as they stopped to examine something. Spencer sniffed. The air raid shelter did not smell of floor wax. The only smell in the place was a faint one of disinfectant coming from either Macarthur's apron or his instruments. Spencer touched the stone floor with his hand: it was corpse-cold and extinct, like a tombstone. Macarthur said slowly and thoughtfully, 'It just isn't the same man when it happens.'

Spencer said 'Pardon?'

Macarthur smiled at him and shook his head at the verification of what appeared to be a fact of great sadness he already knew. Macarthur said softly, reaching inside his apron for a cigarette, 'Death. It just isn't the same person you knew in life.' He took out a package of thick stubby French cigarettes and offered one to Spencer. (Spencer shook his head.) 'I knew him, his name is Superintendent Palmer.'

Spencer had his notebook in his hand. He glanced down the list he had taken from the warrant cards in the dead officers' pockets. Spencer said, 'Farmer.'

'Is it?' Macarthur said, 'Oh.' He lit his cigarette and filled the air with pungent blue smoke, 'He came into the Morgue once with a man's wife to do an identification while I was in the middle of a post-mortem, an autopsy.' Macarthur looked down at the dead, hard face, 'So I covered up the body I was working on and went over to the freezer with him to help him get out the body so the woman—' Macarthur looked hard into the corpse's shocked, staring blue eyes, 'But it was the post-mortem corpse I was working on he wanted and he—' Macarthur's mouth went hard. 'And—' He shrugged. 'He just went straight across to the autopsy table, whipped off the sheet full length where the man's insides were—' Macarthur said with a vehemence that surprised Spencer, 'And that bastard shouted at the woman in Cantonese at the top of his voice as if he was talking to someone who had just committed mass murder, "You! Is this the body of your husband or isn't it?" ' He looked down at the body thoughtfully, 'If one of his Constables – that one there – hadn't been with him I think I would have killed him myself.' Macarthur said quickly, 'And it wasn't a long time ago – not years and years – it was only a couple of weeks ago.' He sounded tight and bitter, 'So maybe you had better write me down in your list of suspects.' Macarthur said with tears glistening in his eyes, 'I don't normally swear, Mr Spencer, but it was the cruellest thing I've ever seen in my life and bastard is the only word to describe him.' He looked down at the body and took the cigarette out of his mouth with a grimace that made it look as if he was tasting poison. Macarthur said to a question Spencer had no intention of asking, 'No, I didn't do it. If I was going to do it I would have done it then.'

Spencer nodded.

'I didn't. I didn't do this—'

Spencer nodded.

Upstairs, the floorboards creaked as Feiffer and Auden must have gone carefully into another room. Spencer said lightly, 'I always thought doctors used arsenic anyway, not bullets.' He tried to smile at Macarthur, but the six uniforms lying in a row on the floor got into his line of vision and, a cold feeling running up his back, the smile turned into a wince. Spencer said, 'Whoever—'

Macarthur said, suddenly professional, 'They appear to have been dead for about five hours. I'll be able to tell you more when I've measured the mean temperature of the cellar in comparison with the rooms upstairs—'

Spencer, his pen poised at his notebook, asked, 'Is that where they were killed?'

Macarthur nodded. The wound he had been examining looked pale and bloodless. 'They were dragged down here after death.' He looked at his watch, 'At about 5 a.m. I assume from a cursory examination on my way in, that whoever killed them then went back upstairs and cleaned up the blood on the floors and walls, which could have been considerable. What killed each of these men was a single projectile that inflicted massive internal bleeding in the region of the right ventricle of the heart and severed the aorta: the main vessel carrying blood away from the heart.' He raised his probe and for an awful moment Spencer thought he was going to pull aside the flaps of torn uniform around the wound and show him. Outside, there was a heavy roll of thunder that echoed against the walls of the room, 'And it wasn't a bullet either.' Macarthur, his mind still moving partially along its own track said reflectively, 'If a doctor wanted to kill someone he'd use poison. The funny thing is that even when the restraints against taking life have been taken away by – by circumstances – in a doctor's mind the restraint against causing unnecessary pain still—' Macarthur said with heavy irony, 'Even in the case of killing someone like Palmer or Farmer or whatever his name was a doctor would find it hard to actually inflict *suffering*.'

Spencer, slightly alarmed, looked down at the body. There was frozen, sharp, terrible pain on the dead man's features. Spencer said quickly, 'Weren't they shot?'

Macarthur said, 'No.' He touched at the wound with his probe, 'And they weren't stabbed either, which was my first thought.' He moved back the wound a little and almost turned Spencer's stomach, 'The entry angle is all wrong.' He indicated the dead policeman who had taken Farmer away from the Mortuary the day of the identification, 'That man there was killed sitting down – according to Mr Feiffer and Auden – in the toilet. For a man to stab at the angle of the wound, at ninety degrees, he would have had to—' Macarthur, indicating another of the row, said evenly, 'And that one there was killed when his back was turned, at the same angle, and he was standing up, and the internal nature of the wounds themselves—' Macarthur said evenly, emotionlessly, 'They all go right through.'

Spencer said for the second time, 'A bullet.'

'—and they have a strange spiralling track, approximately, as best I can tell without dissection of about two turns in six inches.' Spencer caught a whiff of Macarthur's

24

cigarette smoke and felt his stomach turn over. Macarthur said quietly, 'I don't know what killed them, not for certain, but I know if I had been going to do it I wouldn't have done it like this.' He saw Spencer's face and mistook the look there for uncontainable curiosity.

The wounds were all at least an inch and a half in diameter at the body entrances and the same where they exited.

Macarthur said, 'Unlike me, whoever killed them didn't mind inflicting pain in the least.'

Spencer said, alarmed, 'What killed them?'

Macarthur said, 'I don't know.' He held Spencer's eyes as the blue smoke dribbled gently from the corner of his mouth and nostrils.

Macarthur, looking down at the man who had brought a woman into a mortuary in the course of a post-mortem and had produced the ghastly remains of someone she loved as if it was nothing more than a lump of dead, bleeding meat in a butcher's shop, said slowly, 'I don't know.' He listened for a moment to the faint sound of the rain beating down on the roof and windows of the floor above and the sounds of Feiffer and Auden moving around up there where it had all happened, and, moving on to the next body in the awful row, said quietly, 'I just haven't got the faintest idea at all.'

*

In the washroom, gazing at the hole in the plywood toilet door that seemed to terminate against the rear wall in yet another of the deep score marks, Auden said in horror, 'You can't be serious, Harry – *an electric drill*?'

'Have you got any better ideas?' The centre of the deep indentation, on close examination, had yielded up exactly the same as it had yielded up on a cursory examination, namely, nothing. Feiffer said, 'If it was a bullet it would have been still in the plaster. Even if it was a—' He indicated the toilet door with his thumb, 'That hole's almost a circle an inch and a half in diameter. Even with an elephant gun you wouldn't have made a hole like that.' He stepped inside the toilet booth and half closed the door, 'And it's exactly the same size where it went straight through the poor sod who was sitting here. What gun, leaving aside a ship's cannon, do you know that shoots a bullet an inch and a half in diameter?'

'But an electric—' Auden said suddenly, 'This is a washroom. The only power sockets in here are for plug-in razors. You're not telling me that the cat or whatever it was dragged a bloody great oil-drilling sized rig in here, plugged it into a razor socket and then—'

'I'm not telling you anything. All I know is that six cops were killed one after another in this place, from one room to another, and not one of them drew his gun or called out or—' Feiffer drew a breath, 'And if you think the people living on either side of the place are going to report a mass of shouting and screaming in the middle of the night then you don't know the people around here.' Feiffer said hopelessly, 'He must have come in the front door, killed the cop on desk duty, locked the door, and then calmly moved from room to room killing until he came to the toilet, peered under the door, worked out where the cop was sitting and then—'

Auden said, 'A spear. Could it have been a *spear*?' He answered his own question: 'But all the wounds are at right angles, so he—' Auden said, 'So he would have had to have knelt down—' The thought was so Ancient Worldish it bordered on the positively Olympian. Auden said with a shrug, 'So if it was a spear he would have had to—'

'To throw it underarm and spin it at the same time to get it to bore a clean circular hole.'

'But that's impossible!' Auden said aloud, 'A giant cat ... and a butterfly with three wings ... and a ... a what?

26

A cello?' Somehow, without effort in the awful rooms, during the night, six human beings had been slaughtered without a sound. Auden said, 'It has to be a *gun!* What else could it be?'

'*Then where the hell are the spent bullets?*'

Auden said, 'And then, what? He washed and waxed the floor so the blood wouldn't show so he could – what? So he could get more of them as they came in?' He stared hard at the indentation on the wall, the claw mark. 'Harry, when I came in here there was a roster sheet pinned up on the wall of the squadroom. Did you see it?'

Feiffer said, 'Yes. And did you count the names of the people who were supposed to be on duty here last night and today?'

Auden said, 'Well, no. I just assumed, because we found six bodies that—' He asked abruptly, 'How many names were there?'

'Ten.' Feiffer said softly, 'I think, Phil, when The Umbrella Man turned up, the cat or whatever it was was still waiting for the rest of them. For the next shift.'

'But that's—' Auden said, 'But that's— According to Macarthur the six of them had been dead for about – do you mean to say that whatever it was was waiting in here for at least three hours? *With six uniformed cops lying about the place dead?*'

The rain outside was beating down on the roof like wings. Feiffer said quietly, so faintly that Auden had to strain to hear him, 'Unless I'm very much mistaken, Phil, I think whatever it was, the cat, cello, three winged butterfly or spear-thrower – may well have been in here all night.'

The ten names. They had found all the bodies in the station that were to be found.

Auden said, aghast, 'A cop? Are you saying that you think another *cop* killed them?'

'I don't know.' Feiffer said. 'But whoever it was sure as

hell knew where the floor wax and the brooms were kept, didn't he?'

A spear. A silenced gun that conveniently didn't shoot a bullet. An electric drill that ran off shaver sockets, butter-flies, cats, spear-throwers ... Auden said with reluctance, 'Harry, we are assuming that whatever did it—' He looked again, hard, at the holed door and the marks on the plaster and the— Auden said, 'Harry, we are assuming it's *human*, aren't we?'

It seemed a question, sooner or later, someone had to ask.

*

In the rain there was nowhere to go. Singapore Road, like Fade Street, was grey and deserted, all the shops shuttered up tight against the weather, all the street stalls empty and cascading rain into gutters, all the vermillion and blue and white and yellow signs and exhortations to buy, sell, eat, rest or drink sodden and running colours into each other. From his car, Staff Sergeant Shen looked up at windows above the shops: the curtains were all drawn. A bus passed slowly down Singapore Road going in the direction of Yellowthread Street, the driver peering hard through his slashing windscreen wiper and steering careful-ly on the slippery road.

The bus, lit up in the greyness of the day, was empty.

Nowhere to go. Staff Sergeant Shen watched as Police Constable Tong, huddled in a heavy regulation cape, stepped out from a doorway and looked in his direction. Shen's revolver was on the seat beside him. He put his hand on its butt and hefted its weight. He saw Constable Tong see him in the car – probably just as a silhouette – then strain to make out the licence plate.

The revolver in Sergeant Shen's hand gave him confi-dence. Sergeant Shen said softly, 'Yes, it's me all right.

28

Check the number of the car. It's me all right...' He watched as Tong peered out at him from the doorway, his hand under his cape.

Shen said softly, 'Got your gun, have you?' With one eye still on the doorway, Sergeant Shen reached into his tunic pocket for his notebook, flipped it open at the back page, and looked down.

141, Singapore Road. Constable Tong was standing opposite his own apartment house watching.

There was a figure coming down the pavement behind him, dressed in a heavy rain cape and hat: Shen saw it as a moving dissolving blur in his rear view mirror. He twisted to see out the rear window and it was gone.

He looked back to the doorway opposite Tong's apartment house and Tong was gone.

Sergeant Shen said, 'Oh, no—!' For an instant, the figure was in his rear view mirror, moving in the rain.

Shen said, 'Oh – *no!*' Dropping the revolver back onto the seat he twisted at the key in the car's ignition to get it started, panicked and threw the vehicle not into first, but third gear.

It started, coughed, almost died and...

He got the stick into first, rammed his foot down hard on the accelerator and, as the car almost leapt into the air with the sudden unleashed power, had to spin the wheel hard to gain control of it before he could get the wipers on and, in a spume of spraying water, race away to safety in the direction of the waterfront.

He had no idea what was happening. He got the knob of the civilian radio switched on as he turned a corner and listened hard as the announcer, on the hour, read the news.

Nothing.

Nowhere to go.

He felt his heart beating like a trip hammer.

*

At Tropical Cyclone Warning Signal Number Three, shown in the port and waterfront areas as a series of two green and one white light, it was recommended by the Weather Bureau that ships in the harbour seek a safe anchorage. Routinely, ships' masters and other concerned personnel could expect sustained winds of up to 33 knots with the possibility of gusts suddenly exceeding 60 knots. It was further recommended that the owners of premises, at this point, verify and re-secure loose scaffoldings, hoardings and temporary structures, particularly on balconies and roof tops.

Out at sea, the typhoon was moving faster than the satellite pictures had given the weathermen reason to expect. It was veering slightly north easterly and then, in the next picture its centre had turned again and had a slight north westerly direction.

Signal Three, under normal circumstances, gave twelve hours warning of the strong winds to be expected as the typhoon came closer.

This typhoon was moving so fast, building up so quickly, and behaving so unpredictably – even for the most unpredictable class of disturbance it represented – that the strong winds signal was amended both on radio and television to read ten hours.

The weather men looked at the latest satellite picture and the typhoon had turned north easterly again.

At Kai Tak airport, the traffic controllers, in contact with no less than forty eight aircraft of varying size and purpose on their way to Hong Kong, began issuing diversion calls to Bangkok, Singapore and Manila.

The typhoon was hovering a little less than three hundred and twenty miles out in the South China Sea.

Shaking his head, the Chief Safety Officer in the control tower went downstairs to watch the progress of the typhoon on radar and eyeball the deteriorating state of his runways.

Typhoon Pandora. With the lives of two million plus

passengers a year under his control, he failed to see the humour of the name.

All it meant to him was worry.

*

In the air raid shelter, standing back, Constable Yan exchanged a look with Constable Lee and said softly to Feiffer's question, 'No, sir, nobody heard or saw anything.' He saw Macarthur probe at one of the bodies and shut his eyes for a moment, 'We've questioned everyone we could raise in the street and—' He looked up at the cement ceiling as something Macarthur did made a scraping noise and clasped his hands togeher. His voice trailed off, 'No one saw anything...'

By Macarthur, Feiffer said in Cantonese, 'You two can wait outside for the Lab people and the photographers.' He saw Constable Yan touch at his good luck jade ring to ward off the ghosts of the dead men in the room. 'There's no need for you to stay. You can go back to normal duties at Yellowthread Street if you—'

Spencer's face was ashen. Constable Lee saw him swallow hard to keep from throwing up as Macarthur probed the wound. Lee said in English, 'We'll stay, in case you need us. Maybe you might—' He stopped abruptly as Macarthur said with a note of triumph, 'Got it!' He was digging at the body of one of the Chinese Constables. Lee thought he knew him from Training School. Macarthur made a metal scraping noise and said to something at the body, 'I've got it! I've touched something! It's the one from the toilet. He must have put up his hand to protect himself and it's lodged against the side of his wristwatch.' He made a series of stomach turning scraping noises that Lee and Yan tried to tell themselves was only the metal of the long probe touching the metal of the watch. Macarthur said, 'It's a – there are two of them! It's a—' He said as something

31

made a tinkling noise on the ground beside him, 'Razor blades. Two little rectangular razor blades from a—' He looked up at Feiffer in confusion, 'From a safety razor—'

In Chinese mythology the cat was a portent of poverty and hard times, the cat and the butterfly combined portents of death before full, ripe age. Constable Yan twisted his lucky jade and looked hard at Lee.

Macarthur said curiously, 'Two razor blades.' He saw Spencer dutifully taking notes, 'Two apparently stainless steel razorblades of the type inserted in safety razors, about one quarter of an inch in width by approximately an inch in length, single edged, apparently sharp.' He looked up at Feiffer and shook his head, 'Two razor blades.' The wounds were a full inch and a half in diameter, 'That's crazy. What the hell are they for?' He leaned back down to the body and slid his hand in under the dead Constable's back with a lack of hesitation that made Auden look away. His hand came out covered in blood, 'Straight-through wound from chest to back with large exit cavity of at least...' The dead man's hand was lying stiffly at his side. Macarthur raised it an inch with effort against the strength of the rigor mortis and looked hard at the wrist, 'Straight through wound on left wrist of at least an inch and a half in...' Macarthur said, 'This is crazy!' He looked at Auden.

Bullets didn't have built-in razor blades. Auden looked blank.

The razor blades were still lying on the floor, parallel to each other where they had fallen. Feiffer, peering at them, said cautiously, 'Is that some sort of glue on them? On the blunt sides?' Macarthur's tweezers were in his open bag and Feiffer took them out and caught one of the blades and brought it up to his eye, 'It's glue.' The blades were both caked with blood. When they had struck the wristwatch they had sheered off, but cleanly, as if they had been dislodged from something holding them.

Auden said with strained relief, 'Well, at least it wasn't an electric drill...'

Macarthur had the body on its side and the steel probe was digging at something. He said with decision, 'Get hold of his feet and lift him up!'

Auden said, 'Who? Me?'

'Yes, you.' Without waiting he had the dead Constable in the classic under the armpits hold with his body bent to stop the head in case it should loll and as Feiffer moved the two blades to one side on the floor and said to Auden, 'Leave it, I'll do it,' lifted the body up a foot from the ground. Freeing one hand, he paused for a moment, then, reaching in under the body, opened his hand and with a quick upward jerk, gave it a single flat handed slap in the small of the back.

Lee, his mind full of demons and ghosts, said softly to Yan in a Hainan dialect he knew not even Feiffer could understand, 'I don't like this. They don't know what killed them...'

Nothing. Macarthur said in quick explanation, 'I don't want to turn any of them over until the photographs have been taken. This way we can put him back in exactly the same way we—' He slapped hard at the small of the back again.

Nothing.

Macarthur said, '*Damn it!*'

Outside, the thunder was rolling hard.

Feiffer said warningly, 'Doctor, we can't disturb the scene until—'

Macarthur, holding the body with one hand with some effort, said from between gritted teeth, 'It's got to be there, somewhere!' He looked at Spencer watching him, 'If I was going to kill him, by God, I wouldn't have done it like this!' He was beginning to lose control. Macarthur drew back his hand, tensed it, and, giving the dead flesh a final flat blow so hard that the dust billowed out from the blood caked uniform, commanded like a berserk magician, 'Come out, you *bastard*!'

It did. It fluttered to the floor and fell beside the two razor blades lying together in a Vee.

It was a single butterfly wing made of thin silvered tinplate. The dust settled and, a moment later, there fell another.

What had killed the six policemen lay there in pieces on the floor. The two silver wings had landed side by side facing the Vee of the two razor blades. The two razor blades had been embedded in something – in the dim light Auden could see the glue brown and glistening under the blood. Lee and Yan craned closer.

With Feiffer and Macarthur standing above him holding the stiff body like two men about to throw it hard and far into an ocean or over a cliff, Auden took the tweezers and forced the razor blades into a sharp point at the tip of the Vee. The feathers, both cut exactly the same along aerodynamic lines, he moved back about three feet. There was nothing to put between them. The thing or the person that had waited all night in Fade Street for the other four policemen who, for some reason, had not come, had taken that away with him when he cleaned up.

Auden took two long metal probes from Macarthur's bag. (He saw Macarthur nod in permission and approval.)

Each of the probes was about eighteen inches long. He laid them together between the feathers and the blades.

Spencer said softly, from something he had heard or read about a long time ago in boyhood, 'Three feet ... a full clothyard length...'

In the dim, terrible room, with the blood caked hard on its component parts, leaning over it in silence they all saw what it was.

Almost beyond comprehension, it was an arrow.

*

At Kai Tak, the Chief Safety Officer, in the radar room, made his decision and closed the airport runways completely.

With the typhoon coming in fast and the rain increasing hourly in intensity, the Colony was to all intents and purposes, instantly cut off from the rest of the world.

3

The Survival Handbook. SELF SUFFICIENCY FOR EVERY-
ONE

Direct Use of Wind Energy

*... if the area is A square metres and the wind velocity (V) is
measured in metres per second, then the maximum energy passing
through the swept area of a windmill blade is 0.0006 AV³kw ...*

(At his desk, following the words of wisdom with a
raised, waggling finger, O'Yee said, 'Right, right...')

*However, the maximum extractable energy is about 59 per cent of
this figure, and in practice...*

(O'Yee turned the page and said, 'Hmm, practice
– right...')

*...you will do well to extract 43 per cent of the total energy
available in the wind.*

Well, sure, why not? How much did one family need?

*...this giving a usable energy density of only 0.25kw/m² when
the wind is blowing at 8.9 metres per second, because the energy in
the wind is a function of V³, so that the usable energy at 4.45 metres
per second is only 0.3kw/m². Add to it the need to raise the
operating part of your mill above all obstructions and make the
structure holding it strong enough to prevent it being blown down in
gale-force winds and you can see that...*

O'Yee said vaguely, 'Yeah...' He could see that. He went
back to the beginning of the article again and, only pausing momentarily to scratch his head, began re-reading it.

Wonderful, this raw, earthy, back to nature, mountainmen come hard, Noble Savage In Glory stuff. Real, true, plain talkin' information of use to steel muscled, thick calloused, rude souls at peace with nothing but the rocks and the ravines, the wilderness and the woodchucks...

Glancing furtively around the Detectives' Room to check he wasn't being observed, he took his Japanese electronic pocket calculator out of his desk to try to work out what it all meant.

*

On the phone, the Commander said with disbelief, 'A longbow? Do you mean a – *a Robin Hood sort of thing?*' In Macarthur's office off the main operating theatre of the government mortuary, the sound of the cranium saw coming through the door was very loud and Feiffer had to strain to hear the words, 'Jesus Christ, I thought at least it might have been a – well, a bloody *crossbow* or something.' The Commander could also hear the whine of the saw. That and the rib cutters were something you never got used to, 'Do you mean to say that someone carrying a bloody six foot longbow entered that station in the middle of the night and— What the hell else has Macarthur found? A suit of Lincoln Green and the bloody Sheriff of Nottingham's gold medal?'

In the mortuary, all the freezer chests were full with the results of last night's traffic accidents in the rain. The six dead policemen had been put on trolleys around the stainless steel examination table like stretcher victims waiting to be put on board a train. Feiffer said, 'Macarthur's found slivers of wood in the wounds and that combined with the length of two more tinplate vanes he found in Superintendent Farmer's body leads him to believe that the projectile full length, was no less than about twenty eight inches long. The bolt from a crossbow is smaller and it usually only has two steering vanes—'

The Commander said bitterly, 'Thank God for that. Maybe if he'd had a crossbow he would have started by shooting apples off the cops' heads before he killed them.' His voice dropped as the whining of the saw stopped briefly, 'Harry, even at Headquarters there are all sorts of wild rumours about what happened. I'd hoped to hear that it was a mistake and it was some sort of knife or axe or—'

There was a single snap as the rib cutters started their work. In the little room, the pressure of the coming typhoon was building up and taking all the oxygen. Feiffer said acidly, 'I'm sorry to disappoint you.' The six pairs of shoes from the dead men lay in a neat line under a side table holding their wrapped-up and labelled clothing, 'I'm sure they would have preferred it if it had been anything at all.' The saw started again and he looked hard at his notes and read, 'Death appears to have been caused relatively instaneously by a massive severing of the aorta causing violent bleeding into the chest cavity and lungs. In both completed autopsies so far – those of Superintendent Farmer and P.C. Han – the heart gives evidence of having continued to pump for no more than two rhythms after impact and then collapsed, causing death. Distortion of the exit wound suggests that the projectile, passing almost completely through the body and, as the victim either fell or staggered or was pushed against the hard object by the impact, remained in the wound until it was manually removed.' Feiffer said evenly, 'What that means is that the arrowhead hit the walls behind them and made scraping marks on the wall as they fell.'

'The claw marks?' At least that was something real. The Commander said, 'So at least it wasn't a bloody cat. At least that's—' He asked in sudden comprehension, 'What do you mean "manually removed"?'

The smell of lysol disinfectant was strong in the room. Feiffer caught sight of his own reflection in a mirror on the

38

wall of the office. There was a time he had looked as young and fresh as Detective Inspector Spencer. He ran his hand over his thinning fair hair. The face in the mirror looked drawn and tired. Feiffer said, 'It means after he killed each one of them, he calmly went over to them and pulled the arrow out.' He seemed, sometimes, to have spent his entire life, not in the warmth and brightness of the city, but in the presence of the cold, stiffening, stale-smelling dead. Feiffer said evenly, 'Then he dragged them down to the air raid shelter and lined them up in a row, and then he went back into the station, cleaned and waxed the floors so the blood wouldn't show and waited in the darkened room at the end of the corridor for the rest of them to show up so he could do the same to them,' It sounded like a catalogue of almost clinical horror. 'The arrowhead, so far as Macarthur can guess about it from the wound tracks and the razor blades we found, was about an inch and a half in diameter, probably cylindrical in shape with the blades, no less than four of them mounted around it like fins on a rocket.'

The Commander said quietly, 'Oh my God.' He had a press conference called for this morning, 'Anything else?'

'Not so far, no. I've sent Auden and Spencer out to the address of one of the missing cops – a European Inspector called Eason, and two of my Constables have gone to the addresses of a Staff Sergeant and P.C.s Koh and Tong, who are also missing.' There was at least one tiny piece of information that sounded that it might come from the mouth of a rational man or be said in perfectly normal circumstances, 'P.C.s Koh and Tong share an apartment at 141, Singapore Road, and by a coincidence, Sergeant Shen lives in a residential block in the same street, so maybe we'll hear fairly quickly—' The cranium saw hacked hard into bone and he stiffened, 'And—'

The Commander, almost shouting to be heard, said with relief, 'Well, at least it's not a bloody cat! This character,

39

The Umbrella Man, have you got him in the station with O'Yee?'

'He won't go in. I spoke to him again myself when I drove him home.' Feiffer said, trying to force a smile, 'All he seemed concerned about was the dog. I said he could have it.' Anything to drown out the terrible sound of the saw whining and slicing, 'Is that all right?'

The Commander said, 'What dog? Oh. Oh yeah, sure. Either that or have it destroyed.'

'No.'

'What?'

'I said no. If he wants it then I said he could have it.' The sound was growing louder and louder. The smell of lysol and death was everywhere in the suffocating room. There were no windows in Macarthur's office: the light made shadows and patterns on the harsh, undecorated wall, 'I said if he – if he—' The sound was tearing his head apart. Feiffer said, 'Jesus Christ, aren't there enough bloody dead things for one day?'

'*Did you get anything out of him?*' The sound roared like static in the earpiece of the Commander's phone.

Feiffer said, '*No. Only what I've told you! And that his eyes—*' The sound reached crescendo point.

The Commander shouted, '*What?*'

'*And that his eyes—*'

The Commander shouted, 'I can't hear you!' He knew people were listening outside his door. And some god-damned fuckwit, it had said on the radio, had named the coming typhoon Pandora. He had to face a press conference with goddamned dead policemen and longbows and— The Commander said, 'What about his eyes? What about them?'

The saw stopped.

Feiffer said evenly, 'They glittered in the dark.' In the mirror facing him, a tall, tired looking man who around his eyes seemed to have lost all his dreams somewhere along

40

the line, said quietly, 'The man waiting in the darkened room with the longbow, the cat – the Umbrella Man said his eyes glittered in the dark.'

In the next room, having finished with the third body and moved it onto a holding tray, the next rubber-sheeted customer in the queue was wheeled up for consideration.

*

In Singapore Street, P.C. Yan got back into the car dripping wet, took his cap off, tapped it on the dashboard and made it and the floor also dripping wet, and said to Constable Lee, 'Nothing. The desk clerk says Staff Sergeant Shen went off to work early this morning and hasn't been seen since.' Constable Lee had one of his shoes off and was thoughtfully pouring its boatload of water out onto the floor of the car near Yan's capload. Yan said, 'What about you?'

Lee shook his head. Constables Tong and Koh, according to their neighbour, had also left for work early and, similarly according to the neighbour, had not returned. Lee said with his eyes carefully on the floor, 'Were you afraid to search his room?'

Constable Yan nodded, 'What about you?'

Constable Lee looked sheepish.

The rain poured down in a solid grey wall outside the windscreen of their car. The streets were misty and deserted. Yan wound down his window and let the warm drops pour onto his hand.

Checking that their guns were solidly in their holsters and dry, Yan and Lee, putting on caps and shoes, got out of the car wordlessly and, travelling in opposite directions, went back to Shen's residental hotel and Koh and Tong's shared apartment to demand the keys from the building managers and be let in to search.

In the harbour the last of the big ships, a giant,

41

nuclear-powered American aircraft carrier on a goodwill visit, its crew safe and snug below decks, turned ponderously to make its way out to sea to ride out the coming storm.

*

In Inspector Eason's apartment in the government housing block Auden said softly after a whistle, 'Jesus Christ, this place looks like it hasn't been lived in for a week.' The main living room of the small bachelor apartment was so clean you could have done brain surgery on the floor. Auden went into the kitchen and pulled out a drawer. And used the cutlery in there for the instruments. All the windows were closed, the airconditioning humming at low power, everything, including cushions and bed covers in the bedroom fluffed up, arranged neatly, dust free and pristine. Auden said, 'What the hell is this guy – Housewife Of The Year?' He went back into the kitchen and looked for a door to the amah's quarters some of the apartments had. If Eason had an amah – a live-in housekeeper – then she must have got into one of the mouseholes under the floorboards and then, obligingly, not wanting to upset her neat-mad master, filled the mousehole up with plastic wood and pulled the shampooed carpet down over the top of her. Auden called to Spencer in the bathroom, 'Anything in there?'

Spencer came out shaking his head, 'It's all very neat.'

'Neat? Maybe where you come from this place is neat. Where I come from it's bloody spotless!' Auden reached down gently and touched at a cushion on one of the easy chairs. There wasn't even a stain from a TV dinner. Auden asked, 'Do you think he might be queer?'

Spencer said, 'I keep my flat as clean as this if I can.' There was a dimple in the cushion where Auden had touched it. Spencer gave it a tap to take it out. There had been a can of silver polish in the kitchen in the shoe cleaning kit behind the door for, presumably, silver uniform buttons. Spencer said, 'Maybe he just took a pride in his appearance.'

'Well, he hasn't taken a pride in this place for a while.' Auden ran his finger along the top of the airconditioning machine set into one of the walls, 'If he was so neat about everything why did he turn the airconditioning down in the middle of a typhoon warning?' His finger left a faint line of sweat on the metal box, 'This place isn't just clean, it's bloody wiped for fingerprints!' There was a collection of sporting trophies on a side table and, above them, an eight by ten framed photograph of an eager young man in full police uniform, 'Is that him?' Beneath the photograph, the largest of the trophies was for cricket. Auden read the inscription and said with disgust, 'He went to bloody Harrow!'

'Well that explains it. He probably got into the habit of being neat at school and he—'

Auden said, 'You didn't go to Harrow, did you?'

'No,' Spencer said. 'Slough Grammar School.' He gave Auden a shrug and a grin.

'Don't you hand me that stuff. I may be a bloody peasant but I read newspapers. That's a bloody in-joke, isn't it. Slough Grammar School is bloody Eton, isn't it?'

Spencer said, 'I was only there for a while.'

'But they taught you, right, to wipe your fingertips off the bloody airconditioning and everything else after you brushed your teeth – right?'

Spencer shrugged again. He said with yet another self-disparaging smile, 'They should have. Considering some of the villains they've turned out for the last five hundred years or so—'

Auden said coolly, 'I'm not really interested.'

Spencer shrugged.

'And stop bloody shrugging, will you?' He moved the

cricket cup aside with a pencil and gazed at another smaller trophy behind it. It was for the hundred metre dash and it had been awarded by The Gentlemen Of— Auden said with a snarl, 'Christ, it's nice for some people, isn't it?' He picked up the trophy and felt its weight, 'Do you realise this thing is solid silver? Any decent, sensible person wouldn't have it lying around in his flat, he'd have it in the bank so no one could steal it.' There was another, for rifle shooting in the school OTC. That, at least was only plated.

Spencer, defending his kind, said mildly, 'The fact that he went to a good school doesn't necessarily make him—' (Auden said with heavy irony, 'Doesn't it?') 'For all you know, he could have been a scholarship boy or—'

'Were you a scholarship boy?'

'Well, no, but I—' Spencer said with sudden inspiration, 'But it was a sacrifice for my parents to send me there.'

'To bloody *Eton*? What did they have to do – sell off the back ten thousand acres of prime grazing land or let their second gardener go or something? My mother had to scrub floors just to send me to school with bloody shoes!'

Spencer said smiling, 'Oh, I don't believe that...'

If Auden had been wearing his cloth cap he would have used it to smash Spencer's face in with. Auden wrenched open a drawer below the trophies expecting doubtless to find yet more trophies – doubtless solid bloody gold with diamond studs on them – and instead found a bank statement. He couldn't believe the figures. 'Do you know how much this guy's got in the bank? This guy's got a quarter of a million Hong Kong dollars in his account!' He looked hard at the statement, all in black, 'And – Christ – it says up the top that it's only his number *two* account! What the hell has he got in his number *one*?' He looked at the trophies again, 'No wonder he doesn't mind leaving his bloody loot lying around on the table – you could steal the Crown Jewels from this guy and it wouldn't mean as much to him as my bloody lunch money!'

44

Spencer, coming over to look, said reluctantly, 'That does seem like a lot of money for a man who—'

Auden said, 'Who's missing with six of his mates dead in the station.' He rummaged around in the disgustingly neat drawer and found another print out, exactly the same as the first, except for the words ACCOUNT CLOSED stamped across it. Auden said, 'This is graft money. This is money he's grafting from the bloody working class of Hong Kong and now that he's—' The account had been closed eight days ago. Auden said, 'Where the hell's his passport? Or do people like him just buy a bloody plane of their own and—'

Spencer said irritably, 'You don't know it's graft money. You're just assuming. For all you know there could be a perfectly valid reason for his having—'

Auden waved the sheets in front of his face. 'Look at the bloody statements – is that his bloody police pay being deposited each month on this statement? How long's he been at Fade Street? Six months? Seven? Eight? A year? You're supposed to be a bloody detective, look at the photograph! It's a graduating photograph from the Police Training School. See the date? That's six months ago almost to the day. His police pay isn't even listed on this sheet – on this sheet he's been depositing almost forty thousand Hong Kong dollars a month!' There were some things you learned not at staying at Eton but staying at eating. Auden said as if to an idiot child, 'You know, forty thousand Hong Kong dollars: three and a half thousand quid – seven thousand U.S. greenbacks – a *month*! I don't know what the hell you earn, but I don't earn that!'

Spencer said hopelessly, 'Maybe he paid his salary into his Number One account...'

'Maybe he bloody did! Or maybe he used it to wipe his bloody arse on because it was easier than going out and buying bloody toilet paper!' Auden said in a voice thickening with class conflict and wall-shooting at dawn,

'This character's gone. He went back to the station last night to clean up a few loose ends and now, like Lord bloody lucky Lucan, he's buggered off to South America! That's the way the bloody upper classes like him work!'

'No, it isn't! It might have been once, but it isn't anymore.' Spencer, biting his lip, said, 'Just because a man's—' Spencer said softly, almost in an undertone, 'The profound and subtle contest of the spirit with itself...' Spencer said, suddenly deflated, 'Maybe you're right.'

'What are you talking about?' Auden said, amazed, 'You agree with me?' He saw the look on Spencer's face. 'Look, I'm not saying that *you're* not all right.' Auden said magnanimously, 'Some people rise above their background, like me. And you. I'm not saying that you're not all right, because you are. You're a good bloke basically and if you—' Auden feeling rotten said, 'Look, just because he's got the same privileged unfair background that you do doesn't mean that he – I'm not saying he went through Fade Street and actually *committed* the murders, all I'm saying is that—'

The profound and subtle contest of the spirit with itself... It was engraved on the base of a smaller, less ostentatious trophy at the back of the table and it had been won in a town in England called Burnham, dated four years ago.

The Royal Tox, Burnham, England, Awarded to Mr James W. Eason, 14th August Annual FITA Round.

It was a master's award, celebrating the achievement one fine Summer's day the accomplishment half a world away of nothing short of excellence.

A perfect end. It commemorated six exactly dead-centre, pin-hole accurate hits out of six.

The profound and subtle contest of the spirit with itself. It was part of the Great Doctrine of Zen, part of the world-wide and Arcadian ethos to which, the history of its instrument stretching back thousands of years and across all continents,

46

the Royal Tox of Burnham, England, romantically, idylli-
cally and enthusiastically subscribed.

Framed in silver laurel leaves and mounted on its
alabaster stand, restrained in the way that only things of
great and lasting importance can be, it was a trophy for, of
all possible pursuits, Archery.

Basically a good bloke, with a mixture of emotions,
Spencer handed it over to Auden and said quietly,
'Here...'

4

In the Detectives' Room, O'Yee, briefly setting aside his *Boys' Book Of Backyard Camping,* asked as Feiffer came into the room dripping wet, 'Did you have a nice day at the Morgue, dear?'

'Bloody lovely.' With the approaching typhoon, if the humidity in the room increased any more it would be raining in there too. Feiffer said, 'Did you hear from Auden and Spencer?'

'Yeah.' O'Yee indicated Feiffer's moisture glistening desk. 'And Fingerprints and Forensic have been on. So far, they've found no less than one hundred and eight different sets of usable prints and probably twice as many unusable and Forensic have found everyone's footprints and two sets of wild beast marks that they hoped I'd tell them were somebody's sock prints.' O'Yee said, 'So I told them they were Auden's and Spencer's.' He asked, 'Do you know what size shoes Auden takes? He must have feet like snowshoes.' He saw Feiffer put down the report and look at the dampness on his hands with distaste, 'So it's Eason?'

'It looks that way if we assume that someone who's prepared to go to the trouble of waiting in a cop shop all night in some sort of camouflage suit and who's calm enough to pull arrows out of people to hide evidence is also stupid enough to leave archery trophies and bank print outs lying around in his apartment.' Feiffer, picking up

O'Yee's book and glancing at the section telling the youth of America of the joys of the outdoor life, asked, 'Did Lee and Yan get anything from Singapore Road and Shen's hotel?'

'Nothing.' O'Yee surreptitiously turned over the page where it talked about the bracing effect good clean mountain air had on the constitution. You could do worse than have someone like Feiffer busily building your log cabin while you were out tracking game for the table. Feiffer's wife, Nicola, had a degree in pharmacology, so she could be out tracking down medicinal herbs while O'Yee's own wife, together with the kids, could be busily— O'Yee said, 'And before you ask, I've been onto the Sports Council to find out about the local archery clubs and apart from the fact that Eason isn't a member of any of them, the local archery clubs are all off in Taiwan for the Asian Games, and have been for at least three weeks.'

'What about private clubs?'

'There aren't any. The only other people who shoot bows and arrows are, occasionally, the paraplegics.' O'Yee said, 'As the official, anticipate collator in this place, I've had Despatch put out a pick-up message on Eason and the other three if they see them and to cover their home addresses, but if as Auden said on the phone Eason's flat hasn't been lived in for a week it's pretty obvious he's found somewhere safe to go to ground.'

'The place he found to go to ground, according to the roster at Fade Street, was Fade Street.' He couldn't get over the feeling that it was all just a little too pat. 'If Eason had been missing a week we would have heard about it in the circulars. According to the roster he was on duty, perfectly normally. If he wasn't why go to the trouble of chalking his own name in after he's killed everybody?' He said as a sudden thought, 'But he hadn't killed everybody. P.C.s Tong and Koh and Staff Sergeant Shen were still alive.'

O'Yee suggested, 'Maybe he's already killed them somewhere else.'

'Then why put their names up on the roster? He couldn't be so stupid to think that we wouldn't—' Feiffer said with irritation, 'If two or three cops had been missing for even a couple of hours, the Superintendent of the station would have had a radio bulletin out for them. We would have heard about it. And, if not us, North Point. I rang North Point after Auden spoke to me and North Point are as much in the dark about it as we are.' Feiffer said quietly, wiping the damp from his chair with his handkerchief before sitting in it and lighting up what came out of the pack as a soggy cigarette, 'You know, nobody seems to know much about anyone at Fade Street at all, not us, not North Point. The only things I've heard so far about any of them have been about Superintendent Farmer and what I've heard isn't good.' He asked O'Yee, 'Have we ever used any of their people as back-up in one of our operations or anything?'

'No, not that I can think of.'

'Why not?'

O'Yee said, 'We always seem to use North Point Station if we want additional personnel.'

'But Fade Street is closer, isn't it?'

O'Yee shrugged. 'You just never seem to hear much about them. Mind you, they're a uniformed station, there's no detective section—'

'But we've used uniformed people. When I think of it, I just don't seem to ever remember having anything to do with them at all.' Feiffer glanced at the Hong Kong street map on the wall. The map was laid out in red ink in station districts, 'They only seem to have about six streets in their precinct. Are they some sort of hangover from the last re-organisation or something ... or are they Siberia?'

O'Yee said, 'I don't know. I always thought if you were

sent to Siberia you ended up in the New Territories or out on the border or on the old leper colony beat or something. It's not the sort of thing you ask. I don't know.' O'Yee, wanting to change the subject, said with a heavy accent, 'Ah'm jest a man tryin' to find fur bearin' animals to trap for cash.'

So much for that idea. With his eyes still on the map Feiffer shook his head. 'When Auden rang me at the Morgue from what I could gather from his imitation of a downtrodden mass railing against the ruling classes, Eason was some sort of highly-educated, Everest-climbing, steely-eyed son of the Empire type. If that's the case, what was he doing at Fade Street?' He was still shaking his head, 'Any idea whether he passed through police college here? Or was he recruited directly from another force?'

'If he was such a steely-eyed type what was he doing with a quarter of a million bucks in his account?'

Feiffer said, 'His number two account. And an even better question is, why did he close it?' He asked, 'Where are Auden and Spencer now? At Fade Street?'

'Yeah.'

Feiffer said, 'Ring Passport Control and see if anyone with his passport has left the Colony in the last few hours.'

O'Yee shook his head. 'No planes or ferries.'

'Do it anyway. Any time in the last week.' Fade Street on the map was a little like no man's land in the twisting tendrils of streets and alleys. Circled by Singapore Road and Yellowthread Street itself, it looked like nothing so much as a springboard into the deep waters around it. Feiffer said, 'Again, if this character was so bloody brilliant that he could wander through a police station at leisure killing people I can't believe that he'd be so simultaneously stupid as to do it in the onset of a typhoon when he knew there was a better than odds-on chance that as soon as he'd done it the Colony would be closed off and he'd be stuck here.'

51

'What are you going to do? The Commander has been on again—'

Feiffer said quickly, 'I'll be at the University, seeking inspiration.' He looked hard at the map again and, for some reason, the awful sound of the cranium saw seemed to come back to him. He said quickly, 'You, I've also got a job for.' He turned and gave O'Yee a winning smile, 'Right about now, the woods look pretty good to me too.'

O'Yee said, 'Yeah?' He looked down to his book and, for a friend, was even prepared to rip out the odd page so he could take it away with him and study it at his leisure. O'Yee said, 'Those old mountainmen—'

Feiffer nodding, said, '—had true grit, that's what they had.' The winning smile was winning: he could tell by O'Yee's face. Feiffer said, 'Would you do something for me, Christopher?'

'Sure. Anything!'

Feiffer said, 'Mountainman stuff. Not ordinary police work, but real leather skinned, hard knuckled mountain-man stuff—' He shrugged self-effacingly, looked a little embarrassed and, shame-faced, turned away. 'To be honest, something I just don't have the raw nerve for or the—'

Ba'rs, wildcats, death adders, cougars, wild, painted savages – anything! Just give him the chance! O'Yee said, 'Sure! What?'

Feiffer, turning back to face him and getting up quickly to put his coat back on, said quickly, 'Be a pal and ring Internal Affairs would you, and see what they know?'

O'Yee, his face a mask of sudden horror, said aghast, 'Internal Affairs? You want me to ring ... Internal Affairs!?'

Feiffer on his way out said lightly, 'Yes, that's it. I knew you wouldn't mind.' He couldn't hold back an admiring grin, 'You pioneer-types, not only as tough as old boots, but quick too.'

As he went quickly through the charge room towards his

car he heard the fur-hatted old fellow in his cabin say to himself, 'Internal *Affairs*—?!' and thought that, by God, when it came to digging your own grave with your bare hands they just didn't make rawhide tough old-timers like that anymore.

*

Twelve noon. In Fade Street, all the shops and buildings were still shuttered up. From his car, Feiffer glanced over at the driveway to the Fade Street station carpark. Auden and Spencer's unmarked car was parked halfway up the driveway and, on the front door to the station, Feiffer could see the evidence seals and triple padlocks put on by Forensic before they had left.

A quarter of a million dollars and an account number two closed a week before.

A roster listing names of people who were not there.

Somewhere, when the rain stopped and the shops and buildings opened maybe, in the smell of corruption about the place, there would be the answer to *why*.

The rain continued to pour down unabated. Feiffer, setting his windscreen wipers to fast action, turned in the street and went towards the Chinese University of Hong Kong to see a Korean named Kim who he thought might at least be able to tell him *how*.

Storm Signal Six: gale wind expected from the south west quadrant, increasing in force.

Typhoon Pandora, far out to sea, had centered its aim on Hong Kong and, still building, had turned slowly and ominously for the preliminary assault.

*

In the charge room at Fade Street, looking at the chalked-up list of names for the fifth time and comparing them with the fifth different example of handwriting in the Incident And Day book, Auden said, 'Nothing.' The fifth sample of handwriting was that of Jui-hiang Koh, Constable first class, still missing. He turned a page and moved on to the writing, again, of Staff Sergeant Shen. Shen's writing was crabbed, tight, and looked nothing like the bold strokes on the roster board. Auden looked over at Spencer through the open door of the squad room and called out, 'At least this time we can wear bloody shoes.' Not that it made any difference. The whole place had been marked out with white marker tape by Forensic, dusted down by Fingerprints, and looked at hard by Pathology, and pretty much everywhere you walked you weren't supposed to walk anywhere. Auden did a little double-shuffle to avoid stepping on a cardboard sign on the floor reading in English and Chinese, *Scene of Crime. Do Not Disturb* and, then stepping instead on a white marker tape, kicked the sign aside and stood there turning pages in the book.

In the squad room, Spencer put his hand in a drawer in what had been Eason's desk, felt around like a burglar in a safe and came up with nothing. He looked at the palm of his hand: it was clean. Not even dust. Spencer called out, 'Either this man Eason was the cleanest person the Force has ever seen or he—' He reached into the drawer again, felt around at the back, and said, 'Wait a moment.' He pulled the drawer out as far as it would go. Spencer said, 'It's just a twenty cent coin stuck in the joint.'

Auden called out, 'Didn't Eason ever *do* anything around here?' So far, in the course of peering at entries for the last three weeks – a catalogue of car thefts, false burglar alarms, lost cats, dogs, wallets, purses and children – he had found not one entry with Eason's name on it.

Spencer tried a second drawer in the desk. This one looked more promising. It was stuck. He wrenched at it.

It was stuck with a cleaning rag. Spencer called out, 'Maybe he was more administration than—'

'What the hell did he administer – the cleaning staff?' Auden, still turning pages and looking at the roster, said ominously, 'I don't trust anyone who's that neat. It just doesn't sound normal to me.' He came to a new set of handwriting – an entry listing an inventory of storm and emergency equipment and allied stores and, glancing up at the writing in chalk said, 'Got it.'

The entry was signed at the bottom by Police Constable First Class Jui-hiang Koh. Auden said, 'Shit!' Ten cops, six sets of handwriting. He turned over a page and looked at a report listing Lost Property held by the Desk Sergeant, signed, needless to say, by the handwriting he had seen at least twenty times in the book, of the desk sergeant, Shen. Not one entry in Eason's hand. Auden called out to Spencer, 'What the hell was this character Eason, an illiterate?' Something in the station, probably the roof, creaked, and he looked up quickly, saw Spencer had not noticed, and turning to face the room, glancing at the roster sidelong, let go of the big book for a moment and touched at the butt of his gun. Auden called out loudly to Spencer, 'Anything?' The phone rang suddenly on the main desk and he almost jumped out of his skin.

Spencer said, 'No.' He had reached the point of lying full length on the floor scrabbling under the bottom drawer with his outstretched hand. Things sometimes fell down there. He found another coin, amazingly, a little dust, a broken drawer support, got a splinter in his finger, and getting up with a sigh said, 'Nothing. Not a thing. Someone's cleaned out this desk and then wiped it down.' The phone stopped ringing and he called out, 'Who was it?'

Auden said, 'I didn't answer it.' He turned over another page, half listened for the noise again, found an entry signed by another one of the dead cops that looked about as much like the writing on the roster as chalk looked like cheese and said, 'This is a bloody waste of time.' He flipped the book closed, saw for a moment something written on the front cover, and said with triumph, 'Found it!'

The legend written on the cover read:

Fade Street Station, Royal Hong Kong Police.

Monthly Incident And Day Book To Be Held At Front Desk.

Commenced 1st August.

Commencement Authorised By...

Auden looked hard at the signature. No doubt that non-stop scribbler Constable Bloody First Class Jui-hiang Koh.

Superintendent George Farmer, OC, Fade Street.

Auden looked back in the book to the storm equipment inventory and then to the chalked characters on the roster board. Auden said, 'It's Farmer! The writing on the roster board belongs to Superintendent Farmer!' There was a bang as Spencer, back down on his hands and knees scrabbling at yet another part of the desk, banged his head in the knee hole and then the sound of something like adhesive tape being ripped loose.

Auden said, 'Did you hear what I said? It's bloody Farmer's writing—'

Spencer said, 'I've got Eason's passport. It was taped under the desk with a piece of—' He opened the little blue folder carefully and looked at the visa pages, 'There's an entry stamp here showing when he entered the Colony—' He turned back to the first page, 'And the photo matches the one Despatch supplied for the pick-up bulletin and—' Spencer said abruptly, 'It says here his name is Robert John Cartwright.' He looked at the place of issue – London – and the official stamp on the photograph. Spencer read: Place and Date of Birth: London, U.K. 19 July, 1954, Height: 178 cms, Colour of Eyes: Blue, Colour of Hair: Blonde, Visible Peculiarities— Spencer said, alarmed, 'It's the same man but it says here his name is Cartwright.' He looked again at the little photograph in his pocket extracted from Files, 'The File picture from Personnel shows his hair as brown.' There was a typed-in description on the back of the File photo. He read it aloud, 'Height: 5'10", Colour of eyes: Blue, Colour of hair: Brown, Visible Peculiarities...' Spencer said, 'What was he doing with a phoney passport taped under his desk?' Spencer held the passport up to the light, 'Or a genuine one in another—' Spencer pausing, said slowly, 'All the trophies in his apartment were in the name of Eason. Even that training school photo.' He thought back, 'Isn't there anything in the Day Book about him over the last week or so?'

'Only attendance.' Auden was peering hard at the chalked in roster list. 'If Eason was here...' He turned back to the Day Book, 'All the other cops seem to have gone out on jobs over the last week: all the dead ones and the ones who are still missing: P.C.s Tong and Koh and Staff Sergeant Shen – there's nothing about Eason in here at all.'

Spencer, deciding, said, 'This desk has been clean for a week. Nobody could wipe it down so thoroughly if they'd just murdered half a dozen people.' He got down on his hands and knees again, 'There isn't even a scuff mark on the legs where someone sitting at it would have hit it with his shoe.' He ran his finger over the area, 'There's a thin layer of humidity on the wood down there: it hasn't been disturbed for—' The phone rang again and he heard Auden pick it up and say formally, 'Detective Inspector Auden.' Spencer said, musing, 'If Eason was here in the last week why didn't he sit at his desk? And if he wasn't, why did the Superintendent put his name on the roster attendance list?' He glanced down at the passport. A better question was, if he had a quarter of a million dollars and a passport in another name—

Auden said, 'It's the Weather Advisory People. Storm Signal Six has gone up. We have to put the typhoon bars on the windows.' He turned the page in the Day Book to the inventory: *Typhoon Bars: 17, Place of Storage: Under Front Desk, Monthly check done: all correct and in good order.*

Signed by: good old P.C. Jui-hiang Koh.

Auden said, 'I'll do it, shall I?'

Spencer turned the passport over and looked at the back cover. The back, like the front bearing the royal arms, looked pristine, rarely used, and judging from the tape mark still adhering to it, held in place under the desk for a long time.

Auden said, 'I'll do it. It's easy. All I have to do is manhandle seventeen steel typhoon bars into position across seventeen windows so they don't blow in with the typhoon. Nothing to it.'

Spencer saw a faint mark on the back cover of the passport and turned it over and switched on the desk light. Even the bulb seemed to have been wiped clean.

Auden said, 'Sure, leave it to me.' He went to the main desk, dragged out the bars, and made a loud clanging noise.

The faint mark was the outline of something in what glistened in the strong light like oil. Spencer turned the passport around in his hand to catch the reflection of the light.

The outline was something familiar to him, made by something heavy covered in a light film of oil to protect it from rust, something that for some time, maybe in a drawer somewhere had lain on top of the passport before Eason or Cartwright or whoever he was had taken it off and taped the passport safely under his desk.

It was the outline of a Walther PPK 7.65mm automatic pistol. In reverse, in the strong light, Spencer could even read the maker's legend on the slide.

From the next room Auden said suddenly, 'There's an extra window. I've got the charge room typhoon bars and they're marked for each window separately.' He came in carrying a long metal bar with locking devices at each end for affixing to the frame. 'This one says File Room Behind Main Desk, Charge Room, Fade Street. I've looked, and there isn't a file room behind the main desk.' He glanced across the room past Eason or Cartwright's desk to the corner, 'The files are all in here. They've been moved.' He had a torn length of wall paper in his hand. Auden said softly, 'Bill, there's another room in this place, behind the front desk and someone's walled it up.'

Auden said quietly, 'A little earlier, I heard a creaking sound.' He touched at his gun and settled it in his holster. A giant cat with eyes that glittered in the dark, a cello note, a passport in another name for a man with a quarter of a million dollars and a Walther PPK lightly oiled, ready for use.

Auden said ominously, 'I'm not sure, but I think that's where the creaking sound I heard may have come from.'

In the silent, deserted, death-house he saw Spencer touch his fingers to his face and look down at the passport.

*

Even the cross-harbour tunnel linking Hong Kong with the mainland of Kowloon was deserted. Above that tunnel, the harbour was heavy with rain, going dark and grey as the sediment from the ocean floor was stirred up and the rain covered the sun.

With the windscreen wipers off in the glistening humidity of the long underground corridor, his car seemed strangely silent and Feiffer turned up his police band radio for company.

In that empty glistening place, the traffic television monitors watching his progress, the radio waves were suffocated by the weight of water and concrete above him and, passing through Limbo, his car was filled with nothing but a soft, insistent, electronic buzzing.

Somewhere out in the South China Sea Typhoon

Pandora was coming. The tunnel was deserted. All those who could, had fled.

Taking his warrant card from his pocket in readiness for the traffic police at the other end of the tunnel, Feiffer crossed illegally from the slow lane into the fast and, untypically, put his foot down to the floor and speeded up.

5

There was jest one sure way to talk turkey with that thar Internal Affairs lynch mob and that wuz to drag out your old hog's leg Colt before the dark-hearted sons of bitches had time to even put a spitball into the old spitball catcher and blam 'em daid between the bean bags. On the phone, O'Yee, resolved, said, 'Internal Affairs? This is Senior Detective Inspector Christopher O'Yee from Yellowthread Street ringing with the authorisation of Detective Chief Inspector Feiffer *and on behalf of the Commander at Divisional level.*' Eat lead, pardner. O'Yee settled back in his chair with a cigarette hanging out of his mouth and waited for the gasp of fear at the other end of the line.

At the other end of the line there was nothing but silence.

Too much gun? Those old Hawken .58 calibres could cut up a fur bearin' animal pretty bad. O'Yee, taking the cigarette from his mouth and waving it expansively in the air, said, 'It's O.K. It's jest a little plain talkin' is all that's needed.' He put the cigarette quickly back into his mouth and leaned forward again on his desk to look at the list of questions in front of him, 'It's O'Yee at Yellowthread Street. We just want to pull your file on Fade Street.'

There was a sort of whooshing sound on the line.

'Nothing really, um, confidential, just a little background on the place and the officers and an Inspector called Eason...' Still nothing. O'Yee said, 'You know, the one on the APB. You must have heard it on your radios ... the one we want for questioning.' Stubbing out his cigarette nervously O'Yee said uneasily, 'Um, hullo. Internal Affairs? Um, who am I speaking to please?'

Nothing.

There was a click.

O'Yee said, 'Hullo? Hullo?' By God, duped again by some cross-eyed city-bred dude! O'Yee snarled, 'Hey, listen! I'm—'

Very slowly and clearly a voice said in a tone that when Gary Cooper had said, 'Smile when you say that,' hadn't smiled, 'This is Detective Chief Superintendent Arthur Clemenson, the officer commanding Internal Affairs.' (O'Yee said, 'Oh my *God!*') 'If you have anything you wish to say to an officer from this department you may leave your name and address or telephone number and, immediately he is available, you will be contacted. If you feel your message to be too confidential do not speak and try again later.'

There was a click and then, as The Face On The Bar Room Floor looked around for the nearest empty cuspidor to climb into, the entire message was repeated in careful, unaccented, formally correct Cantonese.

Detective Chief Superintendent Clemenson's voice, after another pause, changed back into English, 'There will be a two second tone and then you may speak.'

The faintest of faint voices said in the background, 'It's O'Yee at—' and then as O'Yee said, 'Hullo? Is there anyone there?' there was a single loud tone.

He could swear he heard someone whispering in the background. O'Yee said, 'Hullo? Hullo? Is there anyone listening on the tape? Internal Affairs? Hullo? Hullo—?'

There was a sudden click and a moment before the spool ran out and the line automatically went dead, he heard someone say a single word.

It was 'Eason,' he would have given evidence on oath that it was said by the same voice as the one on the tape

62

and that the tape – the sound of the voice was all wrong – was not a tape at all.

O'Yee dialled the number again.

'...this is Detective Chief Superintendent Arthur Clemenson, the officer in charge at Internal Affairs...'

O'Yee said evenly, 'Commanding. The first time you said "commanding".'

'...um. If you have anything you want to say—'

O'Yee said, ' "Wish." You're not reading your lines properly whoever you are. The first time you said "wish".'

'to, to, um ... or telephone number and—' The voice became hopelessly lost, '...and an officer will ... um...'

In a voice that would have stopped a rampaging Apache dead in his tracks five hundred yards from the ranch house window O'Yee said, 'Internal Affairs? This is O'Yee. *Just what the fuck do you think you're playing at?*'

'This is a taped message...'

'The hell it is! There are goddamned people there playing goddamned stupid buggers and I demand to speak directly to someone in charge—*right now!*' O'Yee said, 'I don't know who you are, but if you're trying to tell me that this is goddamned bloody Jack the Ripper Clemenson then I—'

Clearly, someone in the background said in a gasp, 'For shit's sake, Arthur, you've screwed it up!'

Clemenson's voice said loudly, 'I can't read your fucking writing!'

O'Yee, never pausing, said, '—then I don't believe it because—because—*Arthur?* You've screwed it up, *Arthur?* Arthur ... *Clemenson?*' O'Yee said quavering, '—because— because Mr Clemenson wouldn't treat a brother officer in this manner because he's too—'

Detective Chief Superintendent Clemenson's voice said abruptly, 'Mr O'Yee, this department is temporarily off line for internal calls. I'm sorry to inconvenience you, but we are presently not accepting any—'

'I won't keep you a moment. All I want is for you to send a runner over with a couple of files.'

'I'm afraid that would be quite impossible.'

'Fade Street and Inspector James Eason. All I want is—'

Clemenson said, 'No. I'm afraid there's nobody here at the moment to deal with your request.'

'You're there! You're talking to me!'

There was a pause and then Clemenson said evenly, 'No, Mr O'Yee. I'm not here at all. There's no one here. When you rang up all you got from Internal Affairs was a recording.'

'What the hell are you talking about?' O'Yee said at the limit of his patience, 'Listen, Clemenson or whoever you are—'

The voice turned to steel. 'This is Detective Chief Superintendent Clemenson—'

O'Yee said sarcastically, 'What? In person—or on a fucking recording?'

'On a fucking recording, Mr O'Yee.'

'All I want is—'

Clemenson's voice said in a tone that brooked no further argument, 'On a fucking recording, got that? And that, O'Yee, make no mistake about it, is a goddamned *order!'*

*

In his car Staff Sergeant Shen could hardly believe his ears. Eason. They were after Eason.

'...James William EASON, 27 years, height five foot ten inches tall, weight approximately one hundred and seventy pounds, medium build, eyes blue, European male, possibly wearing police uniform, hair brown. Armed and could be dangerous. Approach with caution. Information to Detectives, Yellowthread Street station, Hong Bay ... May be attempting to leave the Colony by private means. Border watch stations please alert personnel. Waterfront officers to keep watch on small craft leaving harbour. Repeat of preceding message number 45 in the Cantonese language now follows in

64

English: Message Number 45. Wanted for questioning: James William EASON, 27 years, height five foot ten inches tall...

Eason.

They were after Eason.

In his car Staff Sergeant Shen looked down at the gun beside him on the seat.

Information to Yellowthread Street...

They were after *Eason!*

Shen turned off the police band and, without thinking clicked the knob over to a commercial station.

He heard the headlines beginning on the hour and, as he listened, Shen, a missionary-educated Catholic, said over and over, 'Oh my God ... oh Holy Mother of...'

'...where post mortem examinations of the six dead officers are still continuing. Several officers are still missing. Police sources have released their names as Constable First Class Jui-hiang Koh, Constable Second Class F. G. Tong and Staff Sergeant S. K. Shen. The fourth missing officer, named by police as Inspector James W. Eason, a European, is presently being sought for questioning...'

The words fascinated him.

He said nothing, stunned, listening.

He could not believe what he was hearing.

The words blurred into each other and became, finally, incomprehensible.

*

On the phone, the Commander said, 'Forget it.'

'But, sir, we—'

'No, Senior Inspector, just forget it. If there was a recording on the line at Internal Affairs, then there was a recording on the line at Internal Affairs and that's all there is to it.' The Commander said cheerily, 'Listen. Mr O'Yee, lots of people these days use recording machines on their telephones. It has something to do with increased input data and decreased human output potential—or at least that's what I'm told…'

'But sir, there's always someone at Internal Affairs. Internal Affairs can't just close down. It just isn't possible. I told them I had your authorisation to get the files on Eason and Fade Street and everything and they still just—'

The Commander said, hesitating, 'Well—' He said avuncularly, 'Well, don't worry about it at the moment, Christopher. All right?'

Senior Inspector.

Mr O'Yee.

Christopher…

What the hell was going on?

O'Yee said formally, 'Yes, sir, if you say so,' hung up and dialled the number for the Chinese University of Hong Kong to speak to Feiffer.

All the lines across the harbour were temporarily out of action with the rain and all he got from the receiver was a squawking tone that almost deafened him.

Auden and Spencer.

O'Yee dialled the number for Fade Street.

The phone there, still working, rain or no rain, rang and rang and rang.

But nobody picked it up.

*

From a little inside the semi darkened room a voice said pleasantly, 'Ah, Mr Feiffer, I gather from my assistant that you have made the long and wet trip to see me in order to discuss the finer points of the art of killing.' The faceless voice in the gloom asked, 'Is that correct?' The door was opened wide into the room. The voice, moving closer, said welcomingly, 'Do please come in.'

*

In the Detectives' Room the backwoods mountainman schooled in the discipline of solitude and silence, glancing at his wristwatch at the window as the rain poured down unabated, said in desperation, 'Where the hell *is* everybody?'

By the window, a shadow moved, but he did not see it.

It was a van and it drove slowly down the street until it found the ideal place to park and wait.

Inside the van, waiting, there was only a shadow.

Unmoving, patient, unhurried, it was the shadow of death.

In the greyness of the day it seemed to have large, glittering, unblinking eyes.

*

Crouching down in the bushes by the side window at Fade Street, Spencer, getting soaking wet, handed Auden another pebble from the pre-typhoon remnants of some gardening policeman's pride and joy and said mildly, 'Phil, why don't we just clamber up onto the ledge and smash it in with a gun butt or something?' He watched as the accurately-flung stone from Auden's hand was caught by the wind and sailed ten feet high of its mark, and three feet wide, 'Since the window's obviously been painted over it's probably just an old toilet and it isn't going to bother anybody.'

Auden, choosing, this time, his own rock, said tartly, 'It's going to bother me.' Spencer wore a first quality Burberry raincoat that kept him as dry as if he had been wearing duck feathers. Auden's own locally run up in twenty four hours Hong Kong Sieve was about as much use in the rain keeping off business as chicken wire. Auden said, 'It's all right for people like you and Eason or Cartwright or whatever his name is, but people like me have to look out for themselves.' He flung the rock, missed, and undeterred, took up another, 'Internal Affairs are going to be all over this place like a rash as soon as they find out that bloody Eason did it and I'm buggered if they're going to have me up for smashing in police property, old toilet or not.'

Spencer said, 'Then I'll break it.'

Auden looked at him. 'Since when in your childhood did you learn how to make it look like the wind broke a window?'

Spencer said, 'I once broke a window of a neighbour's house with a shotgun pellet.'

'Oh?' The wind was increasing in velocity. Auden selected an appropriately bigger rock.

'Sure. I was after a pheasant with a—' He saw Auden's face and stopped.

Auden said, 'I still haven't finished paying for a car window I broke a few months ago. It's all right for you, you've got a private income.'

'No I haven't.'

'Yes, you bloody have. If you haven't got a private income how come you've got a better raincoat than I have?'

'It isn't mine, it's my flatmate's. He's a Major. He's the one with the private income, not me. I'm as broke as you are.'

Surveying the window from a distance, Auden said with his mind only half on the conversation, 'I'm not broke.' He glanced at the ledge below the window.

Spencer putting his hand on Auden's shoulder said warmly, 'Look, take the raincoat. It's too big for me anyway. I'm just not as well built as you. I'd actually prefer to have yours. It's lighter and—' He saw Auden looking worried, 'Look, you said yourself, people like you rise above your background.' That sounded awful. Spencer said, 'Look, I wish I was you. I wish I was—' It was all hopeless. Spencer said, 'Listen, I heard the noise too. All right? So it's both of us. We'll go up and smash the window in and say we both heard the noise and if Internal Affairs—'

Auden, unconvinced, said, 'Hmm, maybe.' He picked up another stone and glancing again at Spencer's expensive Burberry for confirmation of a life's distrust of the smooth-talking rich, flung it hard, flat, and totally inaccurately at the darkened, pitch black window.

Spencer said encouragingly, 'Here.' The gardening policeman conveniently had fenced his garden in with housebricks. Spencer picked up a brick of his own.

Thrown simultaneously, as Spencer said encouragingly, 'I'm on your side, Phil,' they went through the pitch black window like cannonballs.

*

He saw what he was waiting for. Behind his semi-opaque windscreen he saw what he was waiting for turn into Yellowthread Street and hesitate.

He had been right. He was always right.

He leaned back into the rear of the van and reached out for something, still watching as the thing he had been waiting for looked up and down the full length to satisfy itself about something.

The man with glittering eyes put a glove on his right hand, a cut away thing with only three finger stalls and a wristclip.

He glanced across the road and saw the outline of O'Yee at the window holding a telephone in his hand and dialling a number.

There was a click from inside the van as the man with glittering eyes moved the door lever a fraction and freed it from the locking socket, then, as he settled something across his knees, the sound of a slightly out of tune cello.

The man with glittering eyes waited.

He had parked just in the right place and the thing he had been waiting for was not even aware of his presence.

The man with glittering eyes turned the key two clicks in the ignition and all the ready lights came on on the instrument panel in front of him, oil light, water, battery.

He was ready.

He drew a deep calming breath and, watching through the rain, was ready.

*

Nothing. The little room had been cemented up weeks ago and there was not even a screwed up piece of paper on the stone floor – nothing. Flicking his flashlight into one of the corners and seeing not so much as a mousehole, Auden said, 'Nothing.' He looked at Spencer. 'And now the place is full of bloody housebricks. I hope to Christ one of us knows how to explain that.' He said again, 'Nothing, not even a—' He saw something in one of the other corners and said, 'Look at what we've done to that bloody window frame.' He saw Spencer skulking about in the far corner, bending down at something, and Auden snapped, 'Don't pull that bloody flagstone up! Don't you know anything about the building trade? All those stones are slotted together!' He thought they probably as likely taught carpentry and stonemasonry at bloody Eton as they had given lessons in charge accounts at Harrod's in the miserable dump where he had gone. Auden said, 'You won't find anything under there except—' He saw Spencer's flashlight illuminate something and said in a sudden hush, 'What is it?' There was a growing smell in the dark little room, a heavy fragrance like lilies decaying. The smell became rank and fishy, then stronger, rancid. Auden, coming closer as Spencer slid aside a second flagstone so easily that it could not have been interlocked, said, 'What is it?'

70

He saw Spencer kick aside one of the bricks they had thrown in through the window.

Spencer said, 'It's a grave.'

Auden said softly, 'Christ, Bill, look at his *hair*...!'

*

In Yellowthread Street, with the fast failing light, darkness was only an hour away and, one by one on both sides of the street, all the street lights came on.

The man with glittering eyes had expected it. He was out of sight away from his van and no one saw him waiting.

6

From behind his desk in his book-lined room, Professor Kim, with a self effacing smile, said quietly, 'Mr Feiffer, I am extremely flattered that you have sought me out, but I hardly know where you wish me to begin, and in relation to what subject.' Kim, a Korean, was a very old man, so frail and slight he looked as if, beneath his thin suit, he might at any moment be taken away by the stillness of the air, consumed by it, and be turned into the finest white ash. His head a little to one side, still smiling, he said gently, 'My field is ancient history, the rest—' he paused to choose a descriptive word and found none to fit '—is merely an interest.'

Feiffer said, 'My wife took a course in Chinese Civilization here after she came to the Colony. She mentioned hearing about you.'

Kim said, 'Oh.' He looked at Feiffer carefully. 'But why have you come?'

'To try to get information from you about—'

Kim said with a sigh, 'About the history of the bow and arrow? The bow and arrow is supposed by most authorities to be about fifty thousand years old and probably invented somewhere in Africa.' He raised his fingers in a helpless gesture, then looked down at the little drawing Feiffer had done for him on a sheet of paper on his desk, 'About the remnants of what you believe to be an arrowhead and the flight feathers from an arrow? The arrowhead appears to be made using razor blades for its cutting edges and is based loosely on what could either be the design of a medieval crossbow bolt for hamstringing large animals, a Chinese war arrowhead, or indeed what the Japanese archers used to call a disembowelling arrow.' He gave a little shrug. 'Or it is simply what the maker had to hand and he did the best he could with it.' He looked at the drawing of the metal flights. 'The flights, as you say, are cut from light metal, again like a crossbow bolt design or again—' He saw Feiffer's face. 'There is nothing I can tell you.'

Feiffer said, 'Do you have a bow here, yourself?'

'Yes.' Kim raised his hand in the direction of a little display stand behind him. 'And a collection of arrowheads and various other implements: Greek and Scythian arrowheads, flint arrowheads, one or two English longbow arrowheads, several jade archers' rings and a jade arm bracer from the tomb of a Chinese warrior prince from Szechuan province.' He paused for a moment. 'I owned, briefly, several dated Turkish flight bows and, indeed, a particularly well known bow from Korea, but since I have no family to share my' – again he searched for a word – 'my interest, they have been donated to various museums in and around Seoul.' Kim said, after another thoughtful pause, 'Forgive my ignorance of your profession, Mr Feiffer, but do detectives in Hong Kong carry guns?'

Feiffer said, 'Yes.' There was something strange happening to him. He had felt it all the way up the stairs to the old man's study. He felt somehow uneasy, unfulfilled. For some totally unaccountable reason he said with a grin, 'I've got a friend at the moment who is seriously thinking of giving everything up and fleeing to the backwoods and—' The whole thing was crazy. Feiffer said, 'I think I'm wasting your time.'

Kim, with the faintest of smiles, said, 'No.' He asked, 'What was it your wife said?'

73

Feiffer, embarrassed, said, 'Nothing. Nothing at all.'

'What is it you wish to know?' Professor Kim said abruptly. 'You wish to know nothing about the bow and arrow because you already know as much as I could tell you from your own experts. The information I gave you about the arrowhead you already knew' – he paused for a moment with a strange look on his face – 'And if as a child you made a bow yourself from a stick and a length of string...'

Feiffer said, 'No. I never did. I was brought up here and I—' It seemed in retrospect very odd, '—I never had the opportunity.'

Professor Kim said evenly, 'Mr Feiffer, when people are shot, what do they do?'

'Shot with a gun?' Feiffer said, shrugging, 'Well, they ... they fall over.'

'Always?' Professor Kim leaned forward slightly at his desk, looking interested.

'Well, it depends on where you shoot them.'

'Oh?' Kim thought about it for a moment, 'How do you know that?'

'Well, I—' Feiffer said warily, 'Well, unfortunately, I've—' He said suddenly, 'Are you saying that whoever killed all those people in the station *had done it before?*'

'I am saying nothing.' Professor Kim said, 'All I asked was whether you, as a person who had experience with – various events – would know what would happen if you were to plan to repeat those events.'

'Are you saying the man's a professional killer? *With a bow and arrow?*'

Professor Kim said, 'Now, perhaps you are asking me the question for which you came: is such a stupid little plaything as a bow the weapon of a grown man?'

'Well, naturally, I know it is—'

Professor Kim said, 'Do you? Do you think that if a man carrying a bow and arrow walked into your own police station you would consider the situation so potentially serious that, using your own gun, knowing that your gun had the undoubted potential to—'

Feiffer said, 'No, I wouldn't take him seriously.'

Professor Kim said quietly, 'From what I read in the newspapers, no doubt, in the first instance the policeman who saw him—'

Feiffer said, 'The man at the front desk.'

'—no doubt he failed to take him seriously too.' From somewhere behind his desk Kim produced something in a long leather case, 'Inside this case is a bow. In fact, a Chinese war bow of the late nineteenth century, used during the Boxer Rebellion and belonging to the Museum here.' He asked, 'What is your first reaction to it?'

Feiffer said, 'Curiosity.' He reached out to take the case but Kim pulled it away.

Kim said, 'Why? It is nothing more than a length of very plain wood with a piece of string attached to it at both ends.' He asked, 'Answer me quickly: what image does it cast up in your mind?'

Feiffer, his eyes glued to the long case, said without thinking, 'Power.'

'Your own gun is no doubt considerably more powerful.' Kim, his eyes suddenly bright, said intensely, 'When a man shoots with the bow, it is his own vigour of body that drives the arrow and his own mind that controls the missile's flight. The bow is the first lyre, the monochord, the initial rune of fine art.' He paused, still quoting, his voice firm and unwavering, 'So long as the new moon returns in heaven a bent, beautiful bow, so long the fascination of archery will keep hold of the hearts of men.' Professor Kim said quietly, with a smile, 'That was written by an American, not a Zen Buddhist or a mystic, not even a teacher of ancient history, but I have never heard it said better.' He handed the bow case to Feiffer and watched as he quickly undid the buckle and drew from it a long recurved length of dark-patina-ed wood and sinew. Professor Kim said, 'You have come here with a vague dark longing from the past of your ancestors. You have come here to learn something about the mind of the archer, the man with the bow – the man you fear, who, if you find him, you will be up against with your puny, crude little pistol.' Professor Kim, taking the length of wood from Feiffer's reluctant hand said quietly, 'As a matter of fact I remember your wife. Her name, if my memory serves me, is Nicola and once, with a friend she was in here doing research in my library when I drew this bow to test it.' Holding the bow very gently like a living creature, Kim asked without any trace of vanity, 'Tell me, what did she say about my drawing it?'

Feiffer said quietly, still gazing at the weapon that more than any other all over the world had given barbaric man mastery of the great and previously unconquerable forces that inhabited it, 'She said it was the most beautiful thing she had ever seen in her life.' O'Yee, thou shouldst be living at this hour... Feiffer said, 'Please, would you show me ... how it's done?'

Kim, rising, a very old man holding the long weapon firmly in his two hands and stringing it in a single movement so that the wood and sinew hummed with sudden pent-up primal power, said softly, 'Yes.' Moving to the centre of the long room, he set his feet astride and, drawing a long, calming breath, said in a whisper, 'It would be my delight to do so.'

There was a thick mahogany lectern at the end of the room some thirty feet away, and Kim, reaching down into the bowcase and selecting a long feathered arrow and fitting it to the string, indicated it with an outstretched finger and, for a long moment, stood motionless, contemplating it in silence.

*

Kim said, 'A thought, an idea ... the loosing of the arrow is nothing but...' His entire body was within the bow, the great wood straining and tensing with the power of the string drawn back to his ear. His body was immovable, rock hard, powerful and young. Feiffer saw his eyes bright and yet at the same time glazed with hard, bright pleasure, the arrow feathers like a butterfly, like the birds of the air, held back, poising for the air and sky and freedom, the sharp, shining arrowhead trembling slightly against the belly of the bow, aiming, pointing, ready: man's mastery. Kim said, almost to himself, 'The mind and the body...' Feiffer saw, ever so imperceptibly, his hand on the great bow relaxing, becoming at one with the wood and the motion, his fingers on the shaft of the arrow beginning, ever so minutely, to move, the moment coming, coming...

There was a shattering thump! from somewhere at the end of the room and then the arc of wood and string was gone, the symmetry of man and bent wood changing, becoming still, returning to...

He heard the man sigh, with the lowering bow, for his strength and his youth, and, his mouth gone dry, it was a long time in the silent, timeless room before he could bring himself to look at anything so mundane as the undoubtedly shattered lectern.

A whisper, an echo, something happening from a long time ago.

Feiffer's hands on his lap were still.

It was the most beautiful thing he had ever seen in his life. He looked at Kim's face as he turned to him with the bow still in his hands and, shaking his head, found that, in common shared humanity – the stuff of ancient history that in school he had found so incredibly boring he had wanted to sleep through it – there was absolutely nothing else between them that needed saying.

*

It was a nightmare. A flash of lightning outside turned the unlit walled room slate grey. Auden, holding his flashlight down into the shallow depression under the flagstone looked up and saw dark hollows in Spencer's face. Auden said quietly, 'My God, Bill, he looks like you...' The brown dye had run from Eason's hair in the fermentation of decomposition and the face looking up at him, lifeless, grey and frozen, the fair hair brushed in exactly the same style as Spencer's, was Spencer... Auden said, 'That photo in his flat and the one in his passport, they were blurred...' Eason's hands were at his sides, as if he had been laid out for entombment. Auden said in a whisper, 'My God, it could be you...'

Spencer said, 'Cartwright. The—the photograph of Cartwright in the passport had fair hair.' He put his hands together in front of him and, without being aware of it, pressed them hard together and tried to wipe the clammy perspiration from his palms. Spencer said uneasily, 'No, it's just a superficial resemblance. It's just the hair and the—' Spencer said tersely, 'A lot of people look like me. I've, um, just got one of those faces.' A roll of thunder brought him back to reality and he bent down quickly to the dead man before Auden had the chance to play the beam of light further on the face. 'We'd better—' He looked around for something to do on the body. The light from the flashlight stayed on the dead face, fascinated, around the eyes and hairline. Spencer said, 'There's dried blood here on the tunic in the region of the—' He said suddenly, 'Phil, for God's sake take it away from the face, will you?'

Auden said, 'My God, he could be your twin—'

'Will you please shut up!' It was a nightmare. The whole awful, ghastly place was a single nightmare of silent death and entombment, childhood horror: glittering eyes and cats that – dead men and *(And lo, that dead man was me...)* Spencer said desperately, 'Look, we have to be efficient about it. Look, put the beam on the—' He found his hands

78

were shaking. There was another flash of lightning outside and the room went grey with the light, 'Look, we're grown up adults! We have to—' He said suddenly, putting his hand on the caked tunic and forcing himself to move a flap of it aside, 'He's been dead about a week.' That was a start. Judging by the superficial signs of decomposition – this was Macarthur's job – Spencer said, 'Throw the light on the walled-up door. Judging by the colour of the mortar—' The light began to come back to the face, *Judging by the colour of the mortar—!*' The light went back. Spencer said with relief, 'The door was walled up some time ago.' The light simply wouldn't leave the face. Spencer said quietly, 'Phil, please...' He opened the flap of the tunic and fixed his mind on the wound. There was a mole on the chest. Spencer touched at his own body and ran his fingers over the same spot. 'He's been shot at close range. There's evidence of powder burns.'

Auden said, 'What? Do you mean with a gun?'

'Yes!' Maybe now the light would— Auden got down on his haunches and put the light at last directly on the wound. Spencer said, 'Yes.' His voice was unsteady, 'You can, you can—you can see the powder residue embedded in the tunic and on the surface of the skin.' The entry wound was clear in the beam, 'Some sort of medium calibre bullet that took him in the centre of the chest at relatively close range. A single shot that—' Spencer had his hand flat on the cold alabaster of the skin, 'He's been dead a long time.' He looked down the length of the body to the shoes and then went back to the waist and, gingerly, undid the leather flap of the man's revolver holster. The butt of a .38 Police Positive peeped out, the backstrap shining with humidity and incipient corrosion, 'He's still wearing his service revolver and he—' He patted the tunic pockets. 'His pockets appear to be empty.'

Auden put the torch on the dead man's shoes. 'What's that just above his sock?' He moved down as, in the

79

darkness, Spencer closed his eyes, 'It's an ankle holster.' There was a rustle as he moved the trouser leg up an inch. 'He's wearing an ankle holster.' The periphery of light illuminated Eason's chest and Spencer, still patting at the pockets, felt something hard under the fabric by the left armpit. In the half light he undid a button on the man's tunic and then another on his shirt and reached inside to see what it was.

It was all a single, unspeakable nightmare. Auden said, 'It's a pistol. He's got a second pistol in an ankle holster on his leg.' Auden said with difficulty, trying to lean down to see the butt of the gun without disturbing it for later examination, 'It's a Walther. It looks like—' Auden got the light clearly onto the easily recognisable shape of the manufacturer's product. He could even read a part of the legend on the side. 'It's a Walther PPK 7.65 millimetre automatic pistol.'

There were little shards of plastic inside the shirt, a broken wire, a rectangle of stained adhesive tape, a minute object that looked like some sort of section of a tiny electric motor, and—.

Auden said, 'I can even read the serial number. It's—'

Spencer said quietly in the darkness, 'Phil, this man Eason, or Cartwright, or whatever his name is—'

Auden's flashlight beam came back and illuminated the open chest in a blaze of yellow light.

Spencer said softly, trying not to look any more at the face, 'It looks to me like he's been wired for sound.'

*

There was a slight twang as he tested the bowstring before putting the weapon down carefully on his desk. The cello note. The broadheaded blades of the arrow itself had passed entirely through the inch thick lectern, torn through a second behind it, and stuck fast into the plaster wall behind that. With the faintest of smiles, Kim withdrew the shaft from the wall and looked at the damage. Fortunately, they were old lecterns due for scrapping. Looking down at the razor sharp object in his hand Kim said quietly, handing over the totally undamaged steel broadhead, 'For the technically minded, the bow I was using drew a full eighty five pounds weight – that is the strength required to bring it to its full arc. Such a weight, on record, has killed an elephant with a single arrow. The arrow, when removed from the creature, was found to have penetrated the skull and tissue to a depth of some fourteen inches.' Professor Kim said, 'Since you have told me nothing of the unfortunate men you discovered at Fade Street, I can make no comment, but what does seem likely to me, strictly from my training as an academic used to thinking about the logical, is that, compared to me, your archer is a younger and, no doubt, considerably stronger man.'

He took the broadhead back and gazing thoughtfully at it for a moment, put it carefully and gently onto his desk beside the bow.

Kim said quietly, 'And as such, he would seem to me to be a very dangerous adversary indeed.'

*

INTERPOL TO: ROYAL HONG KONG POLICE, BRITISH CROWN COLONY HONG KONG.
SOURCE: PARIS CRIMINAL INTELLIGENCE COMPUTER. UNSORTED INFORMATION.
REF 11A/967/CAA/1BPH2 MESSAGE FOLLOWS:
ATTENTION: HEADQUARTERS INTELLIGENCE OFFICE
ATTENTION YELLOWTHREAD STREET STATION

ATTENTION: OFFICER IN CHARGE
CALLBACK: CRIM. INT. COMP. OFFICE, INTER-
POL, PARIS
INFORMATION UNSORTED:
YOUR TELEX REPLY: NO (REPEAT NO) INFOR-
MATION USE OF HAND HELD ARCHERY WEA-
PON USE IN PREMEDITATED CRIMINAL ACTIVI-
TY RELEVANT YOUR QUERY CONTINENT OF
EUROPE THIS DECADE. DITTO (REPEAT DITTO)
CONTINENT OF AMERICA DITTO (REPEAT DIT-
TO) CONTINENT OF ASIA.
NO (REPEAT NO) CHOSEN WEAPON PERSON
CONTINENT OF EUROPE, DO CONTINENT
AMERICA, DO CONTINENT ASIA KNOWN TO
FILES THIS OFFICE.
NO (REPEAT NO) PREVIOUS METHOD OF
OPERATION CONTINENT OF EUROPE DO CON-
TINENT AMERICA DO CONTINENT ASIA KNOWN
FILES THIS OFFICE.
NO (REPEAT NO) INFORMATION SIMILAR USE
OF CROSSBOW OR ALLIED WEAPON.
NO (REPEAT NO) INFORMATION SUBJECT
OF—
In fact, nothing. O'Yee looked down to the end of the
tear sheet brought over from Communications by a runner
and began reading the section under ACCIDENTS. It
was a list of little boys who had accidentally or otherwise
put a home made sharpened stick through someone's
prize cow or pig with something made no doubt from
the nearest sapling branch of a tree and the string
taken from one of Mummy's parcels at the corner
store.
SUMMARY: INTERPOL REPORTS NO (REPEAT
NO)...
O'Yee looked up as a shadow at the open door of the Detectives' Room appeared and said, thinking it was Feiffer,

82

'We'd be better off asking them about goddamned—' He said abruptly, '*Koh?* Constable Koh?'

Koh, streaming with water, said simply, 'They've disturbed the grave.' He seemed to be looking hard around the room, trying to find someone, 'I—I saw a newspaper and they're all—' He was shaking his head, 'Where are they?' He seemed unable to understand something, 'They're all dead and they've—'

O'Yee got up to do something. He got up to— He looked down and the chair he had been sitting in had fallen to pieces. The wall behind it had fallen to pieces. There was a hole in the chair and in the wall behind him. Plaster dust was falling down like rain and he—

Koh was on the floor. There was a gout of blood falling down in the air around him. The wall was falling to pieces, the chair was splintering into— *It was all still happening after it had all finished.* Koh was on the ground dead and the blood was still falling down around him as if it was still in the process of happening.

INTERPOL REPORTS NO (REPEAT NO)...

It was all still happening. He was actually seeing the arrow flying out from somewhere inside Koh's tunic and it was passing through his own chair and splintering it and the wall was still exploding in a burst of plaster and powder and the sound was still coming...

Glittering eyes. He was still seeing glittering eyes somewhere outside the door and Koh was still...

An engine. He heard the engine of a car or a van or a truck start.

INTERPOL REPORTS NO (REPEAT NO)...

O'Yee said, 'I—'

INTERPOL REPORTS NO (REPEAT...

O'Yee said, 'I—'

In the street, he heard an engine start.

INTERPOL REPORTS—

The dust and plaster and blood was still falling all around him, like rain.

INTERPOL—

Paralysed with astonishment, he stared down hard at the words on the sheet and, unsuccessfully, tried to work out what they meant.

7

In the Detectives' Room at Yellowthread Street all the desks were glistening with moisture. There was still blood on the floor by O'Yee's desk, mixed in with a fine layer of white plaster dust. On the phone to Internal Affairs, Feiffer glanced through the open doorway to where the ambulancemen were taking Koh's body out into the rain on a stretcher and looked hard at O'Yee watching them. Next to him, Auden and Spencer were waiting to take a statement from him. Feiffer glanced at O'Yee's face. O'Yee, turning in his direction, seemed to look straight through him.

On the phone after a long pause, Detective Chief Superintendent Clemenson said casually, 'Eason, you said his name was? What makes you think he was one of ours?' This time it was not a recording. Feiffer could almost hear him tighten with anticipation, 'So far as I know of anyone called Eason, he was some sort of junior Inspector at Fade Street who—'

Feiffer, still watching O'Yee, said, 'Who carried a hideout gun conveniently strapped to one of his ankles, who had a passport in another name hidden in his desk, who happened to be in the hair dyeing business, and who, wonder of wonders since he wasn't one of yours, had an Internal Affairs standard issue wire recorder hidden under his shirt – presently U/S due to the fact that someone, discovering that he carried all this hardware secreted about various parts of his anatomy, took a dislike to the clinking sound it made when he walked *and put a fucking bullet through his heart!'* In the next room, O'Yee turned away and Feiffer, dropping his voice, said menacingly, 'Listen to me, Clemenson, this isn't Joe Mudd you're talking to, this is someone who less than two hours ago almost had one of his senior officers skewered to the bloody bone by an arrow meant for someone caught up in some dirty little deal you, your man Eason, and, for all I know, the entire strength at Fade Street had cooked up and if you try pulling rank, bloody innocence or – God help you if you do – the old recorded message trick, so help me, I'll come around there, typhoon or no fucking typhoon and make you think the bloody sky has fallen in!' He paused only long enough to see Spencer reach out his hand gently towards O'Yee's shoulder and O'Yee spin around with a look of terror in his eyes. Feiffer demanded, 'The passport was in the name of Cartwright, so which was he? Cartwright or Eason?'

Clemenson said, 'Eason.'

That did it. Exploding, Feiffer roared, 'You lying bastard, there *is* no Eason! Eason is an invention! I checked just one thing – just one – about your friend Eason: about the archery trophy in his apartment because it just so happens that I know someone who has the complete list of members of the Royal Toxophilite Society in England for about the last hundred years and, apart from the fact that he tells me in his professorial way, that trophies aren't awarded for perfect ends by the Royal Tox and further, that on the day the non-existent trophy wasn't awarded the Royal Tox didn't even have a Shoot. He further tells me that no one called Eason has ever been a member of the bloody Royal Tox! Undoubtedly there are copies of the Harrow year books somewhere in the Colony here – even if only in the goddamned Governor's residence – and I'll lay a small bet that if I go through all the names of the old boys in them for the last five hundred years, surprise, surprise, I'll also find that "Eason"—'

'Maybe all you'll find is that he put a fast one over on Recruiting.' Clemenson said unconfidently, 'Maybe all you'll find is that—'

'Maybe all I'll find is that the fast one he put over on Recruiting was so good that they awarded him an Internal Affairs standard issue undercover gun! And then maybe if I ring the Armoury I'll even find that the serial number on that gun even checks out to you! Will I find that? And then maybe if I run the passport he used to get into the Colony through Immigration I might even find that it was one tricked up in the name of Eason by—by who? By the rubberheel mob in London?' Feiffer, lowering his voice slightly as Auden looked around listening demanded, 'Is that where he came from? From C2—from the Serious Complaints Against The Police Office of the bloody London Metropolitan Police?' Feiffer, his face running with sweat in the swelling, explosive atmosphere of the room, said, 'And what should I do then, go to the local bank where he kept his quarter of a million in an open account and ask them who it was transferred to a week ago when it was closed?'

Clemenson, alarmed, said, 'Who told you it was closed a week ago?'

'The goddamned *bank statement* did! It's all that obvious. What did you think, that he'd gone undercover? Is that why you tried to stop my senior inspector from getting the files? Or did you think when he disappeared that maybe he was all set to do a bunk with the dough and so you froze the account before he could touch it?' Feiffer said, 'Listen, Clemenson, you've screwed it up. Whatever little scheme you and Eason or Cartwright or whatever his name was had going at Fade Street has been all, one hundred percent, screwed up—'

Clemenson said suddenly, 'We didn't know *what* happened

to him! Today, this morning, when we heard that every-body in the place had been murdered—'

'They were killed by some maniac with a bow. Eason was killed by a gun and then walled up in the file room *a week ago.*' Feiffer said ominously, 'And if you've thought about it at all, you'll have a fair idea by whom. And now, I want all the reports and files on Eason and whatever he was working on and everything you've got about Fade Street, and I want—'

'Harry, listen—'

Feiffer said, 'No.'

'We can work together on this thing—'

Feiffer said, 'Like hell we can. I've seen the sort of work you do. Hair dye, for Christ's sake! Is that your idea of good deep cover? What in God's name do you do when you just want to insinuate someone into an investigation for just a few hours? Get them to talk with a lisp and hope to God someone might think they're goddamned Bertie Wooster? And all this crap about sporting trophies and good schools and the whole huntin', shotin' and riding garbage, where the hell does that show up in your Boys' Book Of Empire Disguises—in the fucking Gunga Din and Rudyard Kipling chapter? And what the hell have you got so far? That Fade Street was a nest of corruption-taking bastards? That's why they were all sent off there in the first place!' Feiffer, the picture of the dead man being manhandled out through the broken window like a piece of lumber at Fade Street still in his mind, said with undisguised venom, 'This may come as a shock to you but tape recordings aren't admissible evidence in Court unless they're substantiated by—' He said suddenly, 'ICAC. That's it, isn't it?'

Clemenson, too quickly, said, 'I don't know what you mean.'

'I mean: The Independent Commission Against Corrup-tion. I mean, the government appointed watch dogs of the cops and civil servants in this town. I mean—' Feiffer, suddenly seeing it all, said incredulously, 'My God, you people at Internal Affairs haven't got any authorisation for it, have you? This little project hasn't been vetted by the brass from the beginning. This was strictly your own idea to curry a little respect from ICAC by showing them that you were so much on the ball without their help that you even had a man in somewhere like Fade Street and he was—'

Clemenson said, 'I was trying to uphold the reputation of the police! Of us! You and me! I was trying to prove that the police are capable of taking care of their own internal investigations without a lot of over-publicised snoopers coming in from the outside and sending the reputation of every honest cop in Hong Kong straight down the nearest sewer! I was—'

'Then how the hell did you get Eason from C2 if it was all unofficial?'

'That's my affair!'

'And where the hell did you get him a false passport and a PPK if you didn't—'

'The PPK is my own! And Eason happened to be a friend of mine in London – a friend of a friend and he—'

'Are you telling me that he wasn't even a cop? That you recruited him from somewhere else?'

'He used to be a cop! He was a very bright PC in the Met who was thinking of leaving because he couldn't get promotion, and I heard about it and I—'

'*And you got him through Hong Kong Recruiting and had him posted to Fade Street?*' Feiffer said, aghast, 'Are you serious? Have you any idea just how little someone coming from London would know about the way corruption works here? Have you any idea just how little—'

'I gave him a course of instruction!'

'You did what? You gave him what?' It was unbelievable. Feiffer said, 'My God, I've lived here all my life and

I still get caught up even communicating with the Chinese let alone dealing with them. My own officers all speak fluent Cantonese and half the time they—' The pure, egomaniac stupidity of it beggared description, 'One of my officers is half bloody Chinese and even he—' Feiffer demanded, 'And what did he give you? What valuable information have you got for what? Six months work. Is that how long he was at Fade Street? My God, no wonder he had his real passport taped to his desk! It must have been a nightmare for him!'

Clemenson said in an undertone, 'He shouldn't have had his real passport with him. I told him that.'

'Whoever killed him didn't find it, we did! Talk about babes in the wood! They must have seen through him in about ten minutes flat!'

'He got a quarter of a million in bribes in the first six months! That proves something!'

'Are you serious? Even on a good day you couldn't take a quarter that much! Bribes aren't given in money half the time, they're given in favours and overseas properties and—' Feiffer, wiping the sweat and disgust from his forehead, said, 'They put that money through his account so it looked like he had his own personal deal going. Bribe money in a station is shared out. Shared out, even equally among ten of them would have meant no less than two and a half million dollars going through that station every year. Guys who ran the Homicide Squad who got caught for corruption didn't make that much in their entire careers, let alone a newly arrived Probationary Inspector at a ditch water posting like Fade Street!'

'Then where the hell did the money come from? Are you telling me that they were doing a turn-around on him and they were going to charge him with corruption? The people at Fade Street were taking it right and left!'

'Were they? In the time he was there?' Feiffer said, 'I

wonder. I wonder whether, if they were, it wasn't all going to him and they'd all laid off for a while to keep their records clean. I wonder whether every penny didn't go straight into Eason's hands and then straight into yours on record so that when the time came—' Feiffer said quietly, 'Arthur, if this whole deal was unofficial, where did you transfer Eason's account to? Into a police holding deposit or into—'

Clemenson said in a voice so low Feiffer could hardly hear him, 'Into my own personal ... just until Eason came back into the open and... *Those bastards were trying to set up the head of Internal Affairs and they*—' Clemenson said very quietly, 'And they killed him, didn't they?'

Feiffer said, 'Yes.'

'And then they—'

It made sense, but only so far. Feiffer said curiously, 'But to wall him up in their own station?' Feiffer said, 'I don't know. If they intended to knock him off or at least lose him for a while so you'd take personal charge of the money why not...?' If he had found out about Eason that quickly, then the people at Fade Street... Feiffer said, 'What did you get from the reports Eason sent you? Or from the tapes? Anything?'

Clemenson said, 'Nothing. The money was given to him in cash at the end of each month by Staff Sergeant Shen. It was just put on his desk in a sealed envelope and Shen didn't ever say a word.' Clemenson said suddenly violently, 'That bastard Shen even made sure he was wearing gloves at the time! Nothing! That's what we got for all the work! *Nothing!*'

'Did Eason ever mention a grave that had been disturbed?'

'A what?' Clemenson said, 'No, why?'

'According to the officer on duty, when Koh came in here he was raving about a grave being disturbed. I thought at first he must have meant Eason's, but the time's all wrong. When my people were still wondering whether or not to even go around to the side of Fade Street to find the missing window, judging by the amount of rain on his clothes, Koh must have been in the process of walking over here so he couldn't have known. He mentioned a grave as if it had something to do with—' Feiffer said, 'Send over what you've got.'

Clemenson said, ' "The man who sold the future." That's all we've got. Eason once got something out of Shen about the money and all Shen would say was that it was from the man who sold the future.' Clemenson said softly and bitterly, 'So, Harry, it was all for nothing...'

Eason. Cartwright. A disturbed grave. The man who sold the future...

The awful part about it all, since it had happened no less than a full week later, was that the thing that had killed six policemen one morning in Fade Street and another in Yellowthread Street so thoroughly, professionally, and, above all, mercilessly, might have had nothing to do with the death of Eason at all.

Clemenson said quietly, 'Staff Sergeant Shen and P.C. Tong, have you found them yet? Maybe they—'

Feiffer said, 'Yeah. Maybe.' He saw the blood and plaster dust on the floor by O'Yee's desk. In that moment, when the arrow had ripped through Koh's spine and the room had exploded around him, in that moment, outside in the street, seen by nobody, there had been a figure in the rain like a phantom, like a... In the next room, Feiffer saw O'Yee's face.

Clemenson said, 'I'll send the files over.'

Putting his hand to his face, Feiffer said a moment before he hung up, 'Yeah.' He paused for a moment but there was nothing more to say, 'Yeah, you do that.'

He ran his hand over the back of his neck and, taking it away, found it was soaked in perspiration.

*

In the charge room, O'Yee snapped at the limits of his patience, 'All right, Auden, what the hell would you have done? Drawn your goddamned bloody stupid imbecilic magnum like goddamned Billy The Kid and shot him between the eyes? I couldn't even see him! Have you got that? He wasn't even *there!*'

'Well, I wouldn't have just stood there gawping. I would have got out after him into the street and got a shot off at his car or van or whatever it was before he could—'

O'Yee said, 'You don't understand, do you? You really don't ... *dig,* do you? You think what it was was some sort of little plastic bow with a few suction-tipped wooden arrows, don't you? *That fucking thing came in here like an express train!*' He searched for Spencer's face, 'Bill, he doesn't— Listen, Auden, I thought it was a goddamned bolt of lightning! I don't mean that's what it reminded me of – I mean, that's what I thought it was!'

Spencer, touching Auden on the arm said gently, 'Come on, Phil, you can see he's upset...'

O'Yee slapped his head in astonishment. 'Upset? Is that what you call it when someone gets chopped before your goddamned eyes? I wasn't bloody upset, I was bloody—*terrified!* I didn't even really believe it was happening! That thing wasn't like a bullet – it exploded in him like a grenade!' He saw Feiffer standing at the door watching him with a look of concern, 'Harry, these two here think it was some sort of gentle little archery contest and I was sitting down sucking sarsparilla on a bloody deck chair saying, "Oh, jolly good shot" while—' O'Yee said, 'I realise you all think I'm totally bloody bananas about the woods and going native and all the rest of it, but just how in Christ's name do you think that over the last million years or three men went about killing bloody dinosaurs and sabre toothed tigers and—?' He span around to Auden,

'That thing makes your bloody magnum look like a fucking popgun! I didn't even hear a sound, do you realise that? Nothing! Not like in the movies when arrows go whoosh—*nothing!*' He searched for Feiffer. 'Harry, have you ever seen something like that go off? Have you?' O'Yee said, 'Honest to God, it was the most frightening thing I've ever seen in my life! Honest to God, Harry— He exploded. That's all. Koh. He just *exploded.*'

Feiffer nodded.

'He—' O'Yee said with a shrug, 'I thought I was dead. I don't mean I thought it had killed me, I mean...' O'Yee said, 'I thought I was dead and it was something happening in...' O'Yee, looking down at his open palms in a gesture of total helplessness said, 'So help me, I thought I was dead and it was something awful happening in Hell!' His hands started shaking uncontrollably and, a moment before any of them could reach him, he fell down onto his knees and threw up convulsively and helplessly on the floor.

*

On the phone the Commander said quietly, 'Harry, I'm sorry about blocking O'Yee's enquiries earlier, but I've only just discovered from Clemenson that the whole Cartwright/Eason thing was totally unauthorised.' He paused briefly, 'If it's any consolation to anybody, Clemenson's been suspended and—'

In the Detectives' Room Feiffer said, 'I don't know if it's any consolation. Maybe you should ask the family of the boy he sent in there fresh off the boat to get killed.'

The Commander said, 'I have. I've just been on the line to London and I've spoken to my opposite number at Scotland Yard.' He paused, 'He had Cartwright's mother with him and she didn't draw any consolation from it at all. She must have been talking to people at the Yard or she'd had some previous experience with procedure through her son because the first thing she asked me after I'd told her how we found him was whether the bullet that killed him had been matched.' The Commander said, 'Quite a woman. I think, somehow, she was trying to do some honour to her son by asking what he would have asked. I told her it had.'

Feiffer said evenly, 'And you told her which one of them killed him.' Feiffer said ironically, 'Let me guess. It was Farmer.'

'Yes. Superintendent George Farmer.' The Commander said, 'Ballistics checked the murder bullet against the weapons carried by the dead cops as a matter of scene of crime routine and— I told her Farmer was an extremely evil man who her son was trying to get evidence against in order to clear the name of the Hong Kong force against further accusations of corruption. I told her her son was a very brave man and he knew a great deal about the East—' The Commander said in a bitter undertone, 'From, no doubt, his instructional bar room chats with ex-Chief Superintendent Clemenson – and I told her—' The Commander said, 'It was a very unpleasant half hour, Harry, very unpleasant indeed.'

Feiffer said, 'It had to have been Farmer. If it had been anybody else in the station Farmer would have quite happily thrown them to the wolves. He had to be the one who authorised the walling up of the room.'

'Why the hell didn't he just get rid of the body somewhere else?'

Feiffer said, 'Why the hell did he use his own gun?'

'I don't know! Do you?'

'No.'

'And the archer—?'

Feiffer said, 'I don't know that either.'

'And Staff Sergeant Shen and P.C. Tong?'

'They're out there.'

The Commander said bitterly, 'By now, probably dead.'

'Probably.'

'Then what in God's name have we got to go on?' The Commander said with a trace of desperation in his voice, 'I've never used it before, but I do have the authority in certain cases to authorise a shoot on sight order and if you feel—'

'I don't even know what he looks like! One of my officers was probably less than twenty five feet away from him and all he saw was a blur and all he got from the victim before the blur put an arrow into him so fast it was over before it had started was some sort of mad raving about a disturbed grave! Who the hell are we supposed to shoot on sight? A man dressed up in some sort of camouflage outfit carrying a bent bow? A shadow? A goddamned flash of lightning? Who? *Anybody?'*

'I didn't mean it that way! All I meant was that so far, including Eason or Cartwright, eight police officers have been killed in the space of—'

'You don't have to tell us! We've still got the blood on the floor here to prove it!'

'I'm just trying to help!'

'Then help by seeing that idiots like Clemenson stay where they belong – dreaming their mad bloody dreams about bloody life in the Empire in the safety of the nearest public library! That way innocent boys like bloody Eason will get to live to a ripe old age doing what they know about!' Feiffer said, 'Those bastards at Fade Street had all been there for donkey's years. As far as Hong Kong was concerned, Eason or Cartwright or whatever didn't even know how many beans made bloody two! And now he's dead.'

'And so is almost everybody else at Fade Street!'

'Yeah! And I wish to God I thought it was all connected! And I wish to God I knew what disturbed grave Koh was talking about, and I wish to God I knew where Shen and Tong were, but I don't! But I'm sure as hell not going to ring up Scotland Yard or the New York Police Department or someone else whose knowledge of Hong Kong is limited to seeing the latest Kung Fu movie to ask if they'd kindly send across some likely victim for me to send in to find out!'

'Maybe you should have spoken to Cartwright's mother instead of me.'

Feiffer said, 'Yeah, maybe I should have.' He looked across the room at Spencer and saw, for the second time that day, the resemblance between him and the face of the dead man the ambulance team had manhandled out the broken window at Fade Street into the pouring rain. Feiffer said, 'I don't intend to have to ring anybody's mother or wife or anybody else.' The rain outside beat against the window as, out to sea, Typhoon Pandora, totally unpredictably, changed course yet again, 'I intend to keep my people bloody *alive.*'

At his desk, staring down at the caked blood and plaster on the floor, O'Yee, for no apparent reason, said softly, '*God—!*'

What disturbed grave?

What man who sold the future?

Feiffer said firmly, 'But right now, what I'm going to do is send my people home to get some sleep. All right?'

The Commander said, 'Yes. Of course. Yes. Do that.'

Feiffer said, 'Thanks very much.' He glanced across the room and saw O'Yee close his eyes briefly in relief.

*

He was still out there. At sea, Typhoon Pandora veered briefly to the south west and sent rain lashing down against the sides of his van from all four directions at once.

In the darkened cab, unmoving, his eyes watching straight ahead, the archer waited with the steady patience of a hunter and felt neither anxiety nor discomfort.

97

8

...The dogs, who had preceded us in landing, welcomed us in a truly friendly manner, leaping playfully around us; the geese kept up a loud cackling, to which the ducks quacked a powerful bass, while the wild flamingoes responded in unfamiliar notes...

At 6.15 a.m., lying on the sofa in his living room listening to the rain, O'Yee, fully dressed, put his hand to his eyes and said, 'Yeah. Sure.' *The Swiss Family Robinson.* It was one thing to be thrown onto a desert island after a shipwreck and another... Pine Cone Pin. O'Yee said aloud, 'Pine Cone stupid Pin, if he'd had any goddamned sense at all—'

...the latter were in immense numbers, and their voices almost deafened us, especially as they did not accord with the harmony of our civilised fowls. However I rejoiced to see these feathered creatures...

O'Yee said with tears starting in his eyes, 'Bullshit. It's all goddamned bullshit! *Bullshit!*'

...already fancying them on my table, should we be obliged to remain in this desert region...

Pine Cone goddamned Pin. That arrow had gone through Koh like an express train and he had just stood there watching him like—

The phone by his head rang and he picked it up quickly and said, 'Yes?'

It was Harry Feiffer. Feiffer, evidently speaking softly to

98

avoid waking up someone, said, 'Christopher, I didn't wake
you?'

O'Yee said, 'No.'

There was a pause. Feiffer said, 'Are you all right?'

'Yes.'

'I'm ringing from home. I don't want to wake Nicola. I
didn't disturb Emily or—or the kids, did I?'

O'Yee said expressionlessly, 'Nobody knows I'm back. I
was in the living room—reading.'

Feiffer said for the second time, 'Are you all right? Are
you sure everything—'

'Everything's fine.' O'Yee's voice was defensive. He
thought he might say he was sick or that one of the
children... O'Yee said, 'I've got a couple of days leave
coming, Harry—'

Feiffer said with heavy irony, 'Yeah, haven't we all?
Wouldn't it be nice to take one or two of them?' His voice
became brisk, 'Listen, Christopher, I've just been on to the
Duty Officer at Scientific and he gave me a quick verbal
run-down on the half finished Technology report on that
arrow, and it's hand made.'

There was a packet of cigarettes on the table near the
sofa. O'Yee reached over for them and took one out. As he
lit it, his hands were trembling slightly. O'Yee said,
'Yeah?'

'They've done a micro and spectroscope examination on
it and whatever else they do in Scientific and the bottom
line is, leaving aside the length and diameter and the fact
that it's deal hardwood, it was turned, straightened,
tapered, sanded, lacquered, and for all I know christened
with champagne totally by hand.' Feiffer wanted to let the
information sink in, 'It was originally some sort of billet or
piece of wood from a deal table or chair and whoever
turned it into an arrow didn't even use an electric lathe:
they did it, somehow, by a slow, irregular speed hand tool.
Ditto with the head holding the razor blades: it's been

whittled from a piece of ironwood, sanded down to exact shape and then the grooves to hold the blades carefully cut in with a hand held knife.'

O'Yee putting the book on the sofa to one side, said with an effort, 'Real Swiss Family Robinson stuff, isn't it? Just like bloody Robinson Crusoe or—'

'Christopher, are you sure you're all right? You sound a little strange.'

'Do I?' O'Yee said with self recrimination, 'Maybe he's just some fucking maniac who does things the hard way because he wants to prove to himself that he's got the moral fibre to live in the wilds, when in fact he's got about the same speed of reflex and basic grit as a goddamned three-toed fucking sloth!'

There was a pause, and then Feiffer said, 'They found traces of wood shavings and sawdust in minute quantities on the arrow where it rubbed against the bow and in the hand-cut nock on the arrow they found more traces of wax and string fibres. He made the bow himself as well and wove linen into a twelve strand bowstring.' The silence at the other end of the phone made him feel he was talking to himself. Feiffer said, 'And the fact that he suddenly seemed to appear at the station when Koh was there and that he was able to go through the entire Fade Street station room by calculated room without evidently alarming anyone until it was too late—' Feiffer said, 'Christopher, he's a hunter.'

'That's for sure!'

'No, I mean a *hunter*. I mean, that's what he's used to. It isn't impossible to buy deal wood dowels in the Colony, nor, for that matter, woven string. The flights he used on the arrows were cut – with a knife – from tin cans—'

O'Yee said bitterly, 'Bit short of goose feathers was he? He ought to have gone along with the goddamned Robinsons. They had hundreds of them.' O'Yee said evenly, 'Listen, Harry, I've been thinking about things, about myself and—'

Feiffer said, 'He's stalking people. Koh, and Staff Sergeant Shen and P.C. Tong, he's stalking them through the city, Christopher, just as if it was—'

'I don't fucking care any more!' He heard a movement from the bedroom as his wife or one of the children stirred and he dropped his voice, 'All this shit about going out into the woods is just so much shit and if goddamned Pine Cone Arsehole or whatever his goddamned name was had had any real choice in the matter he would have stayed home in bed! I do have a real choice in the matter and there are plenty of safe, easy jobs in Administration that anyone with any goddamned sense—any civilised person—'

Feiffer said over the top of him, 'If he's stalking them, he's probably using everything he knows about their habits to find them, plus any other assistance he can get.' Feiffer said quickly, before O'Yee could respond, 'And that, by now, probably includes us.' Feiffer said flatly, 'Christopher, I think, if he's watching us, it might be a very good idea for us to keep away from our families for a few days.'

...my excellent wife dried her tears, assumed an aspect of composure, and cheered the children, who were clinging around her...

O'Yee said, 'What did you say?'

Feiffer said, 'I'm going to ring Auden and Spencer after I've spoken to you and get them over to Fade Street to go through this man who sold the future thing with the local shopkeepers and businessmen, and I'd like you to try the grave line. I'll take Fade Street's Incident Book and diaries over there together with Internal Affairs' few notes and—'

'What the hell do you mean, he might be after my family?'

'It's possible he thinks we might lead him to Shen and Tong if he can't find them his own way.'

'What the fuck do you mean, my family might be in danger?'

'How do you think he got into Fade Street and knew where everything was in there right down to the broom cupboard? He's a hunter. He's studied the habits of his quarry. For all I know, the only reason he didn't get the lot of them at Fade Street was that, because of the Eason thing – which he probably didn't even know about – Shen and Koh and Tong took one look at The Umbrella Man running from the station and fled before going in.' Feiffer said in a curious tone of voice, 'When I went over to Kowloon to see Professor Kim once or twice I had the feeling someone was following me. I thought it was someone from Internal Affairs, but on reflection—'

O'Yee, his eyes narrowing, listened.

'—on reflection, if it had been someone from Internal Affairs I think I would have spotted them because they're just not that good at following people.' Feiffer said, 'On reflection—'

O'Yee said, 'I'll meet you at Yellowthread Street in about twenty minutes.'

Feiffer said, 'Just go easily and keep an eye out for—'

O'Yee said, 'I'll meet you at Yellowthread Street in about twenty minutes.'

Feiffer said, 'Fine. I'll ring Auden and Spencer.'

'Fine.' There was a silence and then, very gently, O'Yee hung up the phone.

Those old backwoods mountainmen, they had looks in their eyes of steely purpose and hard, unbending—

As he went through the rooms carefully checking the doors and windows O'Yee caught sight of his own face in the reflection on a pane of the dark night outside.

If it was the same look, he did not recognise it from the *Time-Life* picture books of the Frontier, nor from the TV and cinema representations put out from Hollywood.

102

He slipped his blue-steel, fully loaded .38 Detective Special into his shoulder holster, checked it moved freely in the leather, and, like Pine Cone Pin every time he had ventured into the woods to tame a continent, feeling sick to his stomach, went out of his apartment soundlessly, and, checking carefully around him on the stairs, down to his car in the still streaming street.

*

Once, a long time ago, the night floor supervisor at the Peking Road bus station had had a small part in a school play in front of an audience of parents. He had got on O.K., had said his lines O.K., had waited for the answering lines O.K., had nodded or shook his head or whatever the hell it was he had had to do O.K. and then...

And then he had had to walk off the stage back into the wings at a casual, normal, measured, unconcerned pace and his legs had turned to jelly as the entire audience watched every single step and he had known he was walking exactly as if he had something stuck up his arse, and as he had walked the audience had watched every single step and...

Half way across the deserted forecourt of the closed-in depot, the supervisor stopped and touched his fingers together. The tall man in the raincoat with his back to him had his hand resting loosely on the bonnet of his parked camper van and just like the audience...

The supervisor wet his lips and looked around.

The depot was deserted with all the buses taken out of service with the typhoon warnings and there was not even anyone in the closed up snack stalls near the long wooden benches where the passengers normally waited for buses.

The man in the fawn raincoat by the van was watching the supervisor's reflection on the body of his van.

103

He couldn't be: there was not enough light in the early morning sky and, to save power, half the lights in the depot had been put down to dim.

The man's head wasn't even pointing in the direction of the van. It was gazing out at the entrance to the street.

The man knew the supervisor was there. The supervisor had an English Senior Service cigarette in his hand. The man by the van could smell the Virginia tobacco. There was a haze of blue smoke coming from the cigarette. The supervisor looked down at it and dropped it onto the ground and, gently, stood on it and crushed it out.

He saw the man's neck move slightly. He was listening. He had heard the sound.

The supervisor said in English hesitantly, 'Um ... excuse me...'

The voice came out as too soft and awkward. The slight movement in the back of the man's neck was there again.

For some God unknown reason, the supervisor, a Chinese Christian, thought suddenly, 'I've got a family. I go to church and I've got a—' The supervisor, his mouth going dry, said a little louder, 'Excuse me, but all the buses are off.'

Defensive circle: the supervisor had read somewhere or other – in *Reader's Digest* or somewhere – about defensive... The supervisor, keeping well back, said again, 'If you're waiting for a bus...' He found he had his hand clenched hard into a fist by his side. He thought, 'This is crazy. It's just someone standing by a van out of the rain.' He took a step forward and saw the man's head move a fraction. 'Excuse me, but if you're waiting for a—'

The man was standing by a van. Obviously, he had driven in in the van and now he was... There had been people when he was a kid who had totally ignored the supervisor. The supervisor when he had been a kid had had all sorts of important things to say and questions to ask and adults who thought he was less than nothing had simply

104

stared right through him as if he hadn't been there and—
There were still people who did it – the depot manager
and— The supervisor, taking a sudden, decisive step
forward, said loudly, 'You can't park in here and there's an
end to it!' He turned and looked around the depot to see
what the man was looking at. There was nothing, no one,
not a single passenger, floor sweeper, driver, policeman or
even wandering kid in sight. The supervisor said, 'We don't
allow people in here when the buses are off.' The man in
the raincoat turned to look at him and the supervisor,
seeing the steady, unblinking grey eyes settle on him, said
softly under his breath, 'Oh my God...'

The supervisor swallowed and said to the expressionless
face, 'We don't – we don't encourage people to—' He ran
his tongue across his lips. The face was watching him,
waiting, an ordinary sort of face for a European, thin,
tanned, clear-skinned— The supervisor said with an anxious shrug of his shoulders, 'If you're a tourist and you're
lost—' The man's hand was still resting on the bonnet of
the van. The supervisor said with a smile, 'You can't be a
tourist with a van like that. You'd never survive the local
drivers if you—' The face was watching him with a
strange, intense interest. The supervisor said with an
encouraging gesture of his hands, 'You do speak English,
do you?' He could have been a Scandinavian or something.
Scandinavians all had that clear, healthy skin and that
piercing bright look to their eyes from— The supervisor
said, 'Look, I can't stand here talking to you all day. You'll
have to move the van and that's all there is to it.' He
turned and swept his hand around the deserted depot, 'As
you can see, we don't allow people to use this place as a
waiting room when the buses are off. We keep it closed so
we don't get drifters and—' He paused and, after all those
years finally faced the audience to get even, 'Look, I'm in
charge here and in exactly three minutes I'm going to close
the main doors and even if you were the King of the

Goddamned Universe you couldn't get in here! This place is *closed*!'

There was a movement on the man's face, something below the eyes. That bastard was waiting to hear him say it. He couldn't have been. Not like a play where the other actor in the dialogue knew exactly what you were going to say and he was only waiting to hear you say it to be sure it was time for him to say his own lines, but that was exactly what was happening. The man was waiting to hear him say the place was closing! The supervisor saw the faintest, satisfied nod on the man's face as if he had said the lines exactly right and now it was the man in the raincoat's turn and then—

The man in the raincoat said nothing. He stepped back a pace and put his hand on the doorhandle of his van and glanced quickly out into the street. The rain was still falling hard.

The supervisor said, 'Look, um, if it was up to me, I'd let people in, but—'

The man in the raincoat nodded.

The eyes never seemed to leave his face. The supervisor said nervously, 'Well, I won't push you, I'm not closing up for five or six minutes and it is pouring out there and—' He rubbed his fingers over the knuckles of his other hand, 'You know, if you want to—'

The man in the raincoat nodded. His hand moved on the doorhandle and unlocked it with a click.

The supervisor wanted to say, 'Well, I'm—I'm not going to watch you go. You can go without anyone watching you and I—' The supervisor found his hands were shaking and he badly wanted a cigarette. His office across the forecourt was warm and safe and cosy. The supervisor said with a shrug, 'I've got things to do so I'll go off now and I won't—' The supervisor said, 'I won't watch you go—you know, I don't mean to embarrass you in any way, it's just that there are rules and—'

106

Turning, the supervisor thought to say something else, some little thing to...

He made the long walk towards his office with that same strange, awkward stupid walk he had done when he was a kid, the same awful, ungainly conscious walk that had kept him awake for weeks afterwards in tears of embarrassment and—

The man in the raincoat got into his van and nodded to himself. Staff Sergeant Shen and P.C. Tong had been out on the streets running now for over twenty four hours. In his head, silently, the archer was following the running down of their strength and denying them, one by one, their places left to go.

On his way to the office, the supervisor, walking awkwardly, did not turn around once.

If he had, and had tried to read the licence plate on the van, the archer would have had to have killed him on the spot with the hunting knife he carried in his pocket.

But he did not. He went quickly into his office, closed the door, did not appear even for a second at the window overlooking the forecourt, and the archer nodding to himself, put his van into gear and drove carefully parallel with the forecourt out into the rain.

Unlike the supervisor, his mind was uncluttered with memories and he went carefully and directly towards the next spot on his list, the airport, following the route quickly and faultlessly from a folded street map cut into grid sections on the passenger seat next to him.

6.57 a.m. The archer, even in the empty street, put his indicator light on and, legally and carefully, turned left into Yellowthread Street and then, the overhead road signs and rain warning lights a blur in his streaming windscreen, right in the direction of the cross harbour tunnel.

*

Two hundred and sixty miles out to sea Typhoon Pandora was still moving at an estimated eighteen plus nautical miles an hour forward motion. At the airport the Chief Safety Officer tapped at his pocket calculator and divided the two figures. Allowing for a slight veering off to the north west, the typhoon would hit the Colony in approximately eleven and a half hours, during the early evening. Inside the typhoon, the winds were estimated to be moving at approximately one hundred and one miles an hour, increasing in velocity as the swirling mass passed over the sea and dissipated none of its force on the land. From his files the Chief Safety Officer had taken out the Government Commission report into the results of Typhoon Wanda, back in 1962. The Chief Safety Officer, glancing through the graphs showing the Weather Bureau's pressure tube anemometer record registering that at one period during Wanda's passage the wind speeds had reached one hundred and forty knots, glanced down from his office window to the main airport waiting halls and said softly to himself, 'Shit...'

There was one solid mass of people packed into the hall, waiting for flights that would never leave, tourists, impecunious students – in fact anyone who no longer had the price of a hotel to shelter in or anywhere else to go.

The main airport runway was built out into the sea on reclaimed land. The Chief Safety Officer flipped back through the blue cardboard covered report for information on the tide surge. Typhoon Wanda had occured during the hours of daylight and the flooding had been contained so there were no figures. He turned back a page. In 1937 a typhoon had hit, just as Pandora was going to do, during the hours of darkness and the tide wave was estimated to have been thirty feet high. He read the casualty figures and was appalled.

He turned to the Supplement to the report and looked at

108

the pictures. Down in the waiting hall he could see the Airport Police moving through the crowd, stopping from time to time to ask someone for their passport or papers. Two of them, Constables Lee and Sun were from some station on the island, looking so they had said, for two other policemen from the station he had heard about on the news.

They were the least of his problems. For the third time that morning he went across his office and glanced out an overlooking window to check the typhoon bars were all in position on the far side of the viewing windows.

Outside, the rain was still lashing down on the deserted asphalt and concrete runways so thickly he could hardly make out the radar shack at the junction of Runway One and the taxi-ing apron. Grass on the runway verges was held flat by the wind and beyond that he could just see the whitecaps in the harbour and a growing darkness on the faint horizon line between the sky and the sea.

The little radio receiver where he sometimes monitored calls between the tower and incoming traffic was buzzing with faint two-way conversations between distant airports and planes, picked up accidentally in the changing atmospheric conditions. Hong Kong Tower was silent and there was no outgoing or incoming traffic at all.

The Chief Safety Officer, a short service veteran of the Fleet Air Arm, for some reason got a picture in his mind of an aircraft carrier lost in driving fog and rain waiting for launched pilots and aircraft that were wandering hopelessly, never to return. In that aircraft carrier – in his airport – waiting, there were over twelve hundred souls. He looked out at the whitecaps again and the moving, thrusting turbulence of the great currents beneath them.

The casualty figures of hurricane Allen in the Caribbean had gone in excess of almost two hundred people. Some of the bodies particularly in the Haiti and Florida area, he had read, remained still unidentified a year after the event.

He saw a bedraggled looking police officer pass by his open office door and on an inspiration brought on by three years of nailing everything down in the Navy and inventorising it, called out in English, 'Officer, would you ask Public Address to get the passengers to present themselves at the ticket desks so we can verify their identities against the computer printouts?' He saw the officer look a little startled, 'Everybody, including employees and your people. I want a list of everybody in the airport so if the worst happens—' He wondered for a moment at the man's face, 'You do speak English, do you?'

'Yes, sir.' The man turned to go.

The Chief Safety Officer rubbed at his forehead, 'It's just a precautionary measure. You can take the list and printouts around to your Superintendent for safe-keeping.' The Chief Safety Officer, true to naval form, or at least what the long term officers had suggested to him was naval form, tried to make a little joke, 'You never know, you might even find the odd criminal type among them.'

The policeman – the Chief Safety Officer saw by the insignia on his sleeve he was a Sergeant of some sort – said again, 'Yes, sir.' He looked worried.

The Chief Safety Officer said with a shrug, 'It was just a little joke.'

Staff Sergeant Shen, his hand resting on the unbuttoned flap of his revolver holster, paused for a moment. He saw the Chief Safety Officer, looking a little embarrassed, turn back to a printed report on his desk and turn over a few pages to look at a photograph of something.

Staff Sergeant Shen, still hesitating, said, 'Yes, sir. Whatever you say.'

He had a stolen suitcase of clothing out of sight behind him on the floor and, picking it up, he went quickly

110

towards the door to the employees' carpark in the basement of the building to steal a vehicle with a full tank of petrol.

*

7.14 a.m. There was a van pulling into the arrivals area as he drove out and Shen ducked his head as the driver of the van watched him pass.

Shen said in a gasp in English, *'Oh my God!'* His car coughed, made a clicking sound as the hot-wiring slipped, and stopped dead.

Upstairs, the Chief Safety Officer picked up his phone to ask Public Address why the announcement about the names had not yet been made.

The man, wearing a fawn raincoat, was standing by his van deciding whether to go into the waiting room.

Shen said, the car stalled in the street, 'Oh my *God!'*

Two uniformed cops from Yellowthread Street came out of the airport waiting room and looked around for someone. The man wearing the fawn raincoat took their attention for a moment, then as he got back into his van, they dismissed him from their minds.

He knew him.

He knew who he was.

Shen, his eyes staring as he fumbled at the hot-wired ignition of the car under the dashboard, *knew him.*

Suddenly, it all fell into place.

He was the archer and he knew why it had all been done.

He had come back!

Hiding full length on the car seat as the van went by him on its way out again, Staff Sergeant Shen, his hand shaking in terror, worked at the wire linking the ignition and knew that if, somehow, he didn't get the notebooks and records out of Fade Street before someone had the chance to go through them then, one way or the other, undoubtedly, even if the archer didn't get them first, both he and P.C. Tong were dead men.

The man who sold the future.

The car started at the next attempt and, as Shen drove out of the airport in the direction of the cross harbour tunnel to Fade Street, the man who sold the future had very little future left to sell.

9

In the New Hong Bay Cemetery off Great Shanghai Road, after two uninterrupted hours of cemetery-walking, epitaph-reading and generally being soaked to the skin and put in the way of a lethal dose of at least double-pneumonia, O'Yee, huddling for shelter in the doorway of a marble family mausoleum, had been reduced to reminiscing to a pair of stone lions about the good old days.

In the good old days, examining the fine coating of dust and mud and acorn-scrapings on dead P.C. Koh's left shoe, an expert resplendent in a long Ulster and beaten-up tweed hat and liking a good mystery, would have straightened up, put away his pocket magnifying glass and left shoe scraper into a hand made leather glass and scraper holder and, with a smug smile of his craggy, snuff-stained face, said only too knowingly, 'So easy. *Obviously,* since the man had traces of mud, acorn scrapings, and dust on his left shoe *that could have only come from the old Viking grave-yards* at Bluetooth Under Oak, that is where you will find the man has recently been and where, without doubt, you will find the disturbed grave of which he so lately spake.'

P.C. Koh walking in the midst of a pre-typhoon flood, unfortunately for the experts, had had nothing on the sole of his left shoe – or indeed his right – but worn leather and rainwater. And in the centre of the island of Hong Kong with the price of land reaching two million dollars a square inch if there had been any spare Viking graveyards, oak trees, or even mud lying around waiting to get onto the left shoe soles, about thirty years ago some sharp-eyed speculator would have turned them instantly into real estate, table veneer, mud pottery for the tourists and, if he had got a really good deal going, the site of the new Old Viking Graveyard Hilton.

O'Yee, the rain pouring off the tiled roof of the marble death house behind him straight onto his bare head, said bitterly, 'Yeah,' and looked at the stone lions.

The stone lions guarding the little tiled mosaic pathway to the mausoleum, being granite, took no notice of the rain and, like O'Yee, looked as if they were going to be hanging around the New Hong Bay Cemetery until a couple of days before Eternity.

If the rain got much worse they could always amuse themselves by watching the dead rise up and start building arks. Across the twenty-five acre site the rain came down in solid grey sheets and ran in currents along the carefully laid out paths and steps to the various family plots and grave rows.

Mountainmen. Mountainmen buried their friends, comrades, victims and dead Indians down by the river. The Chinese, it seemed, interred the bones of theirs under solid concrete. O'Yee, shaking his head, took up a leather case from the doorway behind him, removed a pair of high powered police-issue field glasses from it and surveyed the place.

Rain. Nothing but rain and concrete. He adjusted the focus and peered through the grey sheets towards the far perimeter of the site to see Aberdeen Road and the waterfront.

Nothing but more rain.

Snuff-Face the Expert said to the assembled open mouthed coterie of admiring Investigators, 'You see, gentlemen, I was on the right track before I had even examined the deceased's shoes because you told me he had no car and I therefore assumed that' – finger raised explanatorily in the air – 'That from whichever graveyard whence he had come, he come that whence by foot *and the New Hong Bay Cemetery is the only graveyard within walking distance.* Ha-ha.'

O'Yee fast disappearing under the rising floor, said bitterly to one of the lions, 'Ha-ha.' Far off on Aberdeen Road he saw car lights and put the glasses on them to see an anonymous looking delivery van of some sort making a careful U-turn in the street with its indicator light flashing.

If a backwoods mountainman was looking around for two missing policemen by now he would have picked up their trail and been tracking them through trackless wastes armed with nothing but his trusty Hawken rifle, his keen sense of smell, and his old skinning knife.

The van halted for a moment in the middle of the street as if the driver was undecided whether to die of exposure and damp or go home to a dry bed, and then, the light still flashing, completed the turn and drove off in the direction of Beach Road.

For all he knew Koh could have been talking about Eason's grave and the fact that he had arrived at Yellowthread Street even before Auden and Spencer had found the walled-off file room could have meant nothing more than he had *assumed* the grave in the file room was going to be disturbed.

If there was a disturbed grave in the New Hong Bay Cemetery then O'Yee couldn't see it.

The man who sold the future. His only momentary consolation was that by now, having even less success than he was himself, Auden and Spencer had probably gone mad in Fade Street and taken to sailing paper boats up and down the running gutters.

115

Feiffer was in the Fade Street station. After Scientific had finished ripping up the floorboards and smashing holes in walls looking for more hidden rooms Fade Street had probably fallen down around Feiffer's ears.

Rain was pouring down in a solid grey mass.

You couldn't disturb a Chinese grave because the Chinese, after they had dried your bones, put you to earth, covered you in about fifty tons of stone, marble and goddamned granite to make sure no one could steal your soul, and then, for good measure shoved a pride of devil defeating lions around the place to be impervious to rain while you were huddling in a doorway getting wet.

Eason had been dead a week before the archer had got into the station. For all anyone knew it had absolutely nothing to do with it.

For all anyone knew, what Koh had been raving about before the archer had got him too in the Detectives' Room could have had absolutely nothing to do with it either. It could have just been—

The van came back and then, far out through the rain at the edge of the cemetery, someone moved.

The brake lights on the van went on and then as the vehicle stopped, off again.

There was a shadow moving at the far edge of the cemetery about three hundred yards away, by the paupers' section.

O'Yee, leaning back a little into the doorway, took up his field glasses and tried to make it out.

The glasses were fogged and all he could see was a blur.

There was another leather case beside the field glasses one, coated in marine varnish to keep out even the slightest trace of moisture. Opening it, O'Yee drew out the scope mounted Remington .223 counter sniper rifle it contained and, removing the lens cap, put it on the moving shadow and then the van.

116

The shadow was P.C. Tong and he was moving stealthily along a pathway looking down at the graves there. A light at the rear of the van came on as the driver started the engine and moved forward.

O'Yee put the scope picture onto the driver and, for the briefest of instants, thought he saw the driver's face.

Rain was pouring off the snarling heads of the twin stone lions in front of him.

Getting up, watching the shadow and the van, O'Yee, putting his hand inside his raincoat and wiping it dry on his shirt, drew back the cocking bolt on the weapon as quietly as he could and, watching carefully as the long, hand-loaded brass shell went with a click into the breech, moved forward silently.

Even with his naked eye he saw the windscreen wipers come on in the van as the driver, having decided on a purpose, surveyed the graveyard methodically and unhurriedly for whatever it was he was looking for.

*

17/8, 2345 hrs. in Temple Street outside No. 26. Crowd of men gambling in the street. Arr. Stn at 00.02 hrs. with 1 Chinese Male under arrest. Ran away and struggled when caught. Exhibits: 4 pieces of candle, 1 broken cup, 2 dice (fish, shrimp and crab), 3 wooden boards, 1 piece of paper with diagrams of fish, shrimp and crab gambling game. Thirty (30) cents cash. Chinese Male I. P. Wong, 25 yrs, res. at 175 Singapore Rd., Hawker. Charged by PC Koh, Staff Sgt. Shen at 0.022 hrs.

18/8, 0223 hrs. Visited SWEDISH MASSAGE SALON at Flat 9, 78 Jasmine Steps Rd. No customers at the time. Spoke to US Naval Shore Patrol in company with PC Tong re report sailors in street causing disturbance. Told Shore Patrol had previously removed two drunken sailors and would speak to prop. Massage Parlour re damage to sign in street.

0245 hrs. Checked report ringing burglar alarm at premises

Kwai Nan Curios in Clark Place and informed key holder.

0312 hrs. In company with key holder premises checked. No sign of entry. Informed alarm company duty officer to turn off alarm as bell cover rusted to housing and could not be undone by myself or keyholder.

0411 hrs. Alarm company employee arrived to turn off alarm...

In Fade Street Station, Feiffer, on the seventy fourth page of P.C. Koh's tightly written one hundred page notebook, rubbed the heels of his hands over his eyes and said softly, 'God...' Beside him on the desk in the squad room next to IA's files and the Incident And Day Book, he had a pile of the little blue pads, each labelled with the name of the dead officer who had carried it. Next to the pile there was a foolscap pad he had brought with him from Yellowthread Street for notes. The pile was half read through and so far the pad for notes was totally bereft of notes.

Eason's notebook would have been nice, but unlike Eason that could have been easily disposed off and by now was no doubt nothing but particles of dust in whatever handy incinerator it had been consigned to.

0516 hrs. Merton Rd. Blue saloon motor car parked illegally at all night taxi rank. Driver, Chinese Male, claimed vehicle had broken down. Strong smell of alcohol. Refused to give his name and was placed in police car. Asked for blood test to prove he was suffering from diabetes and was sober. I said to him in Cantonese, 'If you will give me your name I can take you to the hospital but they will not examine anyone who refuses to give his name.' Told me to commit indecent incestuous act with my dead mother and became violent. I said to him, 'You will do yourself an injury if you struggle in the car.' Took him to St. Paul de Chartres hospital where he was found to have legal alcohol limit for driving and was treated for facial bruising occasioned by hitting his head repeatedly against seat of car.

0601 hrs...

Outside, Feiffer could hear the rain increasing in intensity as the typhoon's cloud walls, stretching out some fifty miles from the eye, moved inexorably closer and closer to the Colony. The roof, like the walls of the building, was creaking and grinding as the weakened structures fought the strain of the increasing air pressure. Some of the floorboards in the squad room were up, making little rat scurrying noises as they buckled and twisted in the heavy moisture. Out in the corridor leading to the rear entrance there was a crash as something fell down and then the smell of dust and floorwax and lysol.

The door to the broom cupboard must have sprung. The smell of lysol reminded Feiffer of the rib cutters in the Morgue and he looked back to the entry on page 74.

...0601 hrs. Hillwood St. corn. Singapore Road. Observed Blue RABBIT motor Scooter travelling without lights. Driver Australian National, Albert J. Tully, China Hotel, Singapore Road, employed Smithson Wire Ropes, HK, Hong Bay. Driving unsteady. Checked licence and vehicle ownership papers. Cautioned to use due care and attention. Said in the English language, 'I am sorry, Constable. It is my birthday and I have had a little too much to drink. I will leave the vehicle here and take a taxi.' Informed he would receive caution in writing. Said in the English language, 'Thank you very much. I will not do it again.'

0716 hrs...

Either Koh at this point had begun to fall asleep with his own mundanity or Feiffer's eyes were giving out. The writing, growing increasingly crabbed with each entry, became positively hieroglyphic.

Feiffer glanced down at the open Incident And Day Book beside him and the entry in Koh's handwriting listing the storm equipment inventory. It was neat, copperplate to a degree that would have delighted the legal profession in *Bleak House* and, as the fortune-tellers from handwriting would have had it, bold, outgoing, confident and forthcoming.

Feiffer turned to the next page. The writing, if anything, became worse. At least it was interesting:

20/8, 0018 hrs. On information received, went to alley off No. 12 Hennesey Road. Discovered remains Chinese Male known to me as P. K. (HERBERT) LING. Evidence of physical beating. Searched pockets in company with staff Sgt. SHEN on arrival Assnt. Gov. Medical Examin. No possessions found. Watch missing. S/Sgt SHEN suggested to Asst. G.M.E. that the deceased appeared to be the victim of a mugger and Asst. G.M.E. replied, 'Not one but several. The victim appears to have a fractured skull and that in my preliminary opinion is what caused death. There are other bruises and contusions on his body.'

Known to both myself and S/Sgt SHEN that the victim was a local hawker of no fixed address with no family. Accompanied body to Mortuary where it was formally identified as P. K. (HERBERT) LING by both myself and S/Sgt SHEN. Advised Station that services of Government Undertaker would be required after post mortem and Inquest as victim had no relatives and informed by SUPERINTENDENT FARMER that this would be done.

The next entry, back to good old boring street police work, was about a lady of dubious virtue and intentions Koh had discovered if not exactly leaning against a lamp post swinging her handbag, then behaving in a suspicious manner as, she had told him, explaining to an inebriated American sailor (evidently one the ultra efficient Shore Patrol had not bundled off to their convenient pokey) the intricacies of telling one Hong Kong banknote clearly denoted in English from another.

The writing for that entry became bold, happy, outgoing and all the rest of it again.

The notepad for notes was still blank. Feiffer, leaning back and stretching, sniffed.

The smell of lysol was overwhelming, mixed in with dry cleaning fluid.

He got up and went into the corridor to close the broom cupboard door and found that one of the lysol bottles had fallen out and broken.

The corrosive lysol was eating into one of the ripped-up floorboards. In the Mortuary where they used that stuff, it went down on tiled floors and stainless steel trays and tables.

He looked around.

There were no tiled floors or stainless stell trays or tables in Fade Street.

Feiffer, glancing through the open door to the roster written on the board in Farmer's hand and then down at the lysol burning on the floor, stopped for a moment.

...advised Station that services of Government Undertaker would be required after post mortem and Inquest as victim had no relatives and informed by SUPERINTENDENT FARMER that this would be done.

Lysol. For floors that lysol would eat into like acid.

The entry about the dead mugging victim had been made on the same day that Doctor Macarthur estimated Eason had been killed. After that entry, the crabbed tight handwriting in Koh's notebook ceased being crabbed.

When they had found the six dead men laid out in the air raid shelter the floors of the station had been waxed clean so anyone entering, before the archer killed them too, would not see the blood and be warned – and so had the air raid shelter which presumably had not been used for forty years and where no one entering would ever come.

Even the naked bulb in the air raid shelter was clean, as if it had been replaced on a regular basis.

And the steel door, when you opened it, did not squeak.

The rain outside, pouring down, made the entire station seem to contract and quiver. Moving quickly to the door of the charge room Feiffer pulled open the air raid shelter door and, switching on the light and seeing before him a stone floor clean to the nth degree, treated no doubt daily with lysol, felt suddenly he was looking over the edge of some dreadful dark abyss, and, ready to cover the blank foolscap pad with notes, knowing now what he was looking for, went quickly back to the squad room and Koh's notes to go through them a second time page by page, looking now, not at the meaning of the words they contained, but at the words themselves.

All he needed was a name and that name, no doubt, belonged to a grave that whoever had employed the archer – or maybe the archer himself – had recently disturbed.

The man who sold the future. Maybe he was the one.

There was a little plastic ruler in one of the desks in the squad room, and taking it over to his desk, Feiffer opened Koh's notebook at page one and began carefully measuring letters and writing down their heights in a column on his notepad, one by one.

*

If he stopped to watch there was a possibility the hot wiring under the dashboard would fail and he might not be able to start it again. At the corner of Fade Street, the car moving sluggishly through the four inches of water swirling out from the backed up drains and gutters, Shen could see at least two detectives' cars: one parked outside the station itself and another – with people in it – opposite outside the fortune-teller's. He had changed his clothes in a public toilet in North Point and he thought if he drove past slowly the cops in the car were hardly likely to recognise him. One of them turned in the front seat of the car, wound his window down and pointed at something, then looked irritated, wound it up again shaking his sleeve dry in the general direction of the man next to him.

Shen knew him: Auden from Yellowthread Street.

The other car parked at the station was empty. There was the faintest glow coming from inside the station and he knew that at least one more of them was in there, by now already in the air raid shelter working it out.

Staff Sergeant Shen had his police notebook clutched hard in his hand. By now they would have P.C. Koh's notebook and like that clever cunt Koh himself, they would be working it all out.

He was always the bright one, old P.C. Koh, always the one volunteering to show off his fluent command of English and his beautiful script and his beautiful—

And now the stupid bastard was dead. Shen said under his breath as the car moved slowly through the water in the road, 'Really clever, Koh, really fucking brilliant. You work out why everyone got killed and so the first thing you do is rush off to Yellowthread Street to give yourself up and turn Queen's Evidence to save your own skin.' It had been on the car radio how the archer had almost killed Senior Detective Inspector O'Yee along with Koh. Shen said bitterly, 'Really clever, Koh, you conniving little—' He saw Auden glance over in his direction as he passed by and, following good police procedure, seeing that the citizen inside showed neither undue interest nor undue lack of interest, look away again.

With the two cop cars in the street, dealing with the man who sold the future, for the moment, was out. What he had to do was—

The car coughed and he jammed his foot hard down on the pedal and pumped petrol into the ailing, water clogged engine. It caught.

What he had to do was be as clever as Koh and— He passed the police station. It was grey and empty-looking, somehow ailing, looking as if it was only a dead shell that—

Only he and Tong were left to tell the tale.

Without Tong everything that happened in there was just guesswork.

Farmer was dead, and Eason, and Koh and all the others and without someone left to tell the tale everything that had happened that night was nothing but the word of a few shopkeepers, a mass murder, and a pile of guesswork.

There was no evidence in the air raid shelter and there never had been (the lysol had seen to that) and if in the course of almost a full six months of poking the IA spy Eason had come up with exactly nothing, then the chances of a few people from Yellowthread Street bumbling and guessing around the place and meeting a wall of silence from the shopkeepers...

He was home dry! It hadn't occured to him before that he was home dry. Without P.C. Tong it was all just suspicions and guesswork.

Without Tong, no one could ever be sure what had happened, and as for his own part, even if they got him and interrogated him, he was a cop himself and he knew all the tricks and he would simply bluff it out and no one would ever be sure.

Without Tong, he was home dry!

P.C. Tong...

P.C. Frederick Tong...

P.C. Frederick Tong of the limited intelligence...

He could kill Tong.

And that would be the end of it.

Reaching the end of the street Shen wound down his window and began ripping out the pages of his notebook one by one against the pressure of the steering wheel. He could say he had left his notebook in the station and when he and Tong and Koh had come on duty a little early that morning and seen The Umbrella Man fleeing the place in terror they had been so frightened they had simply panicked and run away.

124

He could say that. All it would make him in the long run was a very rich coward. And it was true. That was exactly what had happened.

The only difference was that he had thought The Umbrella Man had somehow stumbled onto another beating or seen Farmer unwalling the file room to remove Eason's body and he was running not to the nearest phone, but straight to Internal Affairs.

He could say Tong and Koh were responsible for the beatings and Farmer for Eason.

He could say...

The truth, or a censored part of it, would make you free.

But it would make Tong dead.

He had kept his service revolver. He couldn't say he had thrown that away. If he was caught that would sound too suspicious. He would have to strangle Tong or beat him to death with something.

That part of it was easy. He had done it once before and he knew how easy a fatal beating up really was if you knew just where to hit someone.

The grave. P.C. Tong had to be at the grave.

Staff Sergeant Shen nodded to himself.

He smiled. After all, the grave was the only place P.C. Tong had left to go.

He turned the car in the direction of the waterfront and, pumping the pedal to keep the engine alive, set about making a systematic plan of execution.

*

...advised Station that services of Government Undertaker would be required after post mortem and Inquest as victim had no relatives and informed by SUPERINTENDENT FARMER that this would be done.

And then, because he had stopped writing out the entire 74 pages of the notebook from page one, the crabbed

125

writing had stopped, and the next entry on the next day after he had gone home and rested from his labours, was in P.C. Koh's beautiful round calligraphy of even, not diminishing, letter heights again.

After the man called Ling had been found dead Koh had come back to the station and – no doubt on Farmer's orders – destroyed his old notebook and rewritten the history of the Fade Street Soviet to fit in with the current historical truth that the man Ling had been killed in an alley by a gang of muggers.

He had been killed by a gang all right, but the gang lived not in alleys but in a police station and he had been killed right here in the air raid shelter washed daily with lysol. And Eason had walked right in on it, no doubt reached for his hide-out automatic in his ankle holster, got no further than the first movement of his hand, and died on the spot with Farmer's bullet in him.

P.K. Herbert Ling. If he had been stripped of everything he owned, how did Koh in his notebook – and no doubt Shen in his exact duplicate – know a wristwatch was missing?

On Chinese skin, especially in a hot climate where a watch was often taken off or worn loosely, there was never any mark where a watch had been worn on the wrist.

P.K. (HERBERT) LING, hawker. If the cops at Fade Street were as officious and efficient as their notebooks suggested then they either knew Ling as a hawker because (a) he was licensed and they often stopped to speak to him in the street, or (b) because he was not and they often had him in the pokey on charges.

The air raid shelter door was made of steel, unused, theoretically, for more than forty years, and yet the light bulbs had been changed regularly and the door, when pushed, swung easily, smoothly, and lightly on well-oiled hinges.

126

Taking up the telephone on the charge room desk Feiffer rang the number for the Computer Room at Criminal Records and Administration at Police Headquarters and asked a single question.

Hawker, licensed or otherwise, there was no such person as P. K. (HERBERT) Ling.

...advised Station that services of Government Undertaker would be required after post mortem and Inquest as victim had no relatives and informed by SUPERINTENDENT FARMER that this would be done...

...and Asst. G.M.E. replied, 'Not one but several. The victim appears to have a fractured skull and that, in my opinion, is what caused death. There are other bruises and contusions on the body...'

It was a torture chamber and the archer, when he had gone through the station, had taken them down there through the well-oiled door and laid them out on the lysol clean floor in a row, one by one.

An awful thought struck him and with the wind outside increasing in ferocity and shaking at the weakened building and flickering the lights, Feiffer said softly to the open door of the air raid shelter, '*My God, how many times have they done it before?*'

*

The van had gone, disappeared into the greyness. O'Yee saw the lights of another car coming through the rain, turning into Aberdeen Road from somewhere farther along the waterfront.

P. C. Tong was a little in front of him, a blur in the rain. O'Yee heard a sound coming from him and then words in Cantonese.

Over and over P. C. Tong was saying to the grave in front of him, 'I'm sorry. I swear I'm sorry. It was Shen and Koh and Farmer...' He had some little thing in his hand, a

127

page from a notebook with Chinese characters drawn in on it in thick pencil, and he was pushing it against the tomb marker and offering it to the spirits.

He was on his knees in front of the grave with his free hand pressed against his face.

There were three characters drawn in on the sheet of paper: a name.

O'Yee could hear him.

Past help, his head and shoulders running with water, between the words, he was weeping.

10

There was a pool of water spreading around Auden's shoes on the floor of the car and a pool of perspiration spreading around his neck and chest with the weight of the raincoat that kept the water off. Sitting next to Spencer in the passenger seat of the car he flapped his raincoat, eased the flood of perspiration, and sprayed Spencer, also flapping with water, onto his so far water-free shirt.

Every one of the establishments in Fade Street selling anything was boarded up, shuttered and inaccessible, and if anyone had sold his future the transaction for today must have taken place yesterday.

Double Satisfaction Mak. Water Mirror Too Good To Be True Fortune Teller. Rates on application.

Auden glancing up at the painted sign on the window of a Sam Spade like office above a camera store facing the police station, said still flapping, 'It's the wrong place. It's the man who sold the future, not he man who tells it.' It was the only business, judging by the light glowing in the window, that seemed to be still in business.

Spencer looking up at the sign, shrugged. It was the last place left in the street they could try.

Auden warming to the argument said with a raised thumb to put the place in artist's perspective, 'And if he's such a hot fortune teller anyway what the hell's he doing telling fortunes? If he was as good as his sign says all he'd have to do is tell the future long shot at Happy Valley racecourse, put his bundle on it, and then—'

Spencer said, 'Fortunes, not future. There's a bit of difference actually.'

Auden said, 'Crap.' He had had experience of the occult. 'Listen, I knew a girl once in England who was big on fortunes. She did it with cards—'

Spencer said, 'The Water Mirror is an ancient volume about—'

'Four of them. She'd deal you three of them and tell you what the future had in store for you.'

Spencer said, '—physiognomy.'

'It's all the same bloody thing! This girl, I remember one time she dealt me four cards, right? This'll tell you all you need to know about fortune telling: the nine of Diamonds, which means: take a chance, it will pay off. Right? The ace of Spades' – he checked to see he still had Spencer's attention – 'which means: problems ahead, *don't* take a chance. The three of Clubs, which means: you will change your mind about something, and last – the big kicker in the juice, the big pay-off, the four of Spades *which means be careful whose advice you take!*' Auden said, stopping flapping and opening his hands in easy conquest, 'See, it's all crap.'

Spencer said, nodding, 'Sure.' He flapped some of Auden's water from his shirt.

'But you don't believe me, right? We've spent the entire morning going up and down this bloody street banging on doors and getting nowhere and now you want to finish off the whole stupid bloody shambles by consulting a fortune teller who tells fortunes, not the future and please does he mind not making it too bloody obvious that he thinks we're completely around the twist.' Auden said, 'O'Yee's been issued a counter-sniper rifle. That's the sort of job I should be doing, not all this!'

Spencer said, 'Maybe he might know what the man who

130

sold the future means. In any event, everything else is closed.'

Auden said with a snarl, 'Double Satisfaction Mak ... I know the Water Mirror fortune by physiognomy bit. I went to one of them before the senior inspector's exam. He told me I was the Ox Type.'

Spencer said, 'Really? I didn't know you believed in that sort of thing.'

'Fat lot of bloody good it did me since I failed the bloody thing!' Auden, glowering, said, 'What are you—the bloody Phoenix Type?'

'What's the Phoenix Type?'

'That's the one with the bloody aristocratic countenance and favourable implications! And the bloody Ox Type—'

Spencer said helpfully, 'I realise, Phil, that in Chinese mythology the Ox doesn't necessarily mean slow and stupid the way it does in the West—'

Auden said, 'Yes, it does.' Auden said, 'I'm off fortune tellers so if you want to ask him if he knows who the bloody man who sold the future is then you ask him and as soon as he starts on the bit about who's your Ox Type friend I'm going to—'

Spencer said, 'I'll do all the asking.' He could see Auden was upset, 'We'll just go across, bang on the side door and if there's anyone there I'll just show them my warrant card, ask him if he knows, and if he doesn't we'll come straight back to the car and call it a day.'

Auden said, 'Bloody soaking wet.' He got out of the car into the rain and stood there looking up at the sign with a look of disgust on his face.

Spencer the Phoenix Type, seeing him hesitate, came over to the other side of the car and patted him on the shoulder. Spencer said with a smile, 'Look, it's probably the wrong place anyway. Maybe you tried the senior inspector's exam without enough preparation. Nobody's saying these people actually know the future for you.' He

131

led the way to the side door and banged on it loudly above the rain to be heard, 'Nobody has any good idea from one moment to the next what's going to happen to anybody.' He nodded, the Phoenix Type at home in any situation, and said to Auden, getting soaked through his still open raincoat, to encourage him, 'Right?'

Wrong. The fortune teller who opened the door to them, a short balding little man wearing thick glasses, had a very good idea indeed. Cradling an enormous 10 gauge duck shooting shotgun expertly in his hands he lifted the twin barrels up in a single movement that located them squarely amidships of both Auden and Spencer in the narrow doorway and, his face twisted in venom, said in a single rasped out command in English, *'Murdering, stinking bastards, get in here and die on the floor like slugs!'*

*

The most important thing in life for a Chinese was to be buried properly. In the Fade Street charge room Feiffer turned the pages of the Station Incident And Day Book until he came to the entry he was looking for and read without surprise: 'Staff Sgt. Shen, P.C. Koh: Body of Chinese Male, approx 50 years, discovered alley off 12 Hennesey Road. Identified under P.K.(HERBERT) LING, hawker, of no fixed address. Remains removed to Mortuary under supervision Asst. Govt. Medical Officer. Evidence robbery, evidence death by severe beating, person or persons unknown.' Shen's writing, and under it in another's – (Koh's): 'See Coronial Inquest report 567/23–8/3. Verdict recorded: Felonious killing by person or persons unknown in course of robbery', and then, far below it at the bottom of the page, another entry: 'Page 45 this Incident Book accidently made illegible by ink stains. I certify that this is a true copy of page 45 (numbered serially) of this Incident Book, seen by me.' And then a name signed at the bottom of the page

132

over a rubber Station stamp: *Supt. G. Farmer, RHKP, O.C. Fade Street Station, Hong Kong.*

They had even rewritten the page in the Incident And Day Book and had the man who had killed Eason sign it in his best hand complete with rubber stamp. Perfect. In the creaking station Feiffer shook his head and made a bitter smile.

Eason they probably intended to simply disappear from the attendance reports a few weeks later or when IA started making enquiries about him. Eason with his quarter of a million Hong Kong dollars and his unauthorised, improbable mission to spy out a nest of vipers in a police station.

It was perfect.

P.K.(HERBERT) LING. The most important thing in life for a Chinese was to be buried properly. *...services of Government Undertaker would be required as victim had no relatives and informed by SUPERINTENDENT FARMER that this...*

They had consigned Ling whoever he was to a pauper's grave and sent his spirit into the next world without his true name. Bastards beyond words, all of them, even Shen and Koh and Tong and the rest of the Chinese officers who would have known, they had tortured and beaten his body until it was dead and then, not even satisfied at that, they had rewritten their notebooks and taken pages from the Incident And Day Book and irrevocably and deliberately sent his soul pseudonymously into torment for eternity.

P.K.(Herbert) Ling. The disturbed grave would bear that name.

But why? What had he done? P.K.(HERBERT) LING... Unemployed hawker of no fixed address with a wristwatch missing that no one would ever have known was there in the first place. P.K.(Herbert) Ling of Coronial Inquest Report 567/23–8/3, all finished, zipped up nicely, put out of the way, disposed of, sent into the next world – and forgotten.

...as victim had no relatives and...

In the charge room under the flickering lights Feiffer said suddenly, 'Like hell he didn't!'

One of them, or someone paid by one of them, had come into their little, secure, all zipped-up, rubber stamped little world and, one by one, working silently with a weapon ideally suited for the job, once and for all, had paid them back and left their corpses in their own charnel room with the well-oiled steel door.

Someone with glittering eyes, a phantom from that other world where P.K.(Herbert) Ling's soul shrieked in torment had come and dealt with them.

Someone...

Someone with glittering eyes in the darkness and rain had waited for them, waited and killed, waited and killed, waited and then washed away the blood and then killed some more.

Staring hard at the rubber stamped redone page in the Incident And Day Book, Feiffer said softly, 'But who? Who?'

P.K.(HERBERT) LING, hawker, of no fixed address...

There was another entry that began at the bottom of the page, almost covered by Farmer's signature and stamp, listing the possessions found on the body:

Handkerchief.....1

Small change.....total $1.60 (one dollar and sixty cents)

Match.....1

Wristwatch.....None

Wallet.....None

Rings.....None

Identification.....None

Other Personal Items or Objects.....None

Clothing: (the list went over onto the next page)

Underwear.....items 2 (cotton, white)

Shirt.....1 (tailed silk, cream)

Trousers.....(cotton, fawn, tailored)

Belt.....None

Socks.....1 pair (nylon, fawn)

Tie.....None

Shoes.....1 pair (leather. brown)

Other Items.....None

Blood group found on clothing.....victim's own

Other forensic evidence.....None

Dentures.....Not applicable

Wig.....Not applicable

Other cosmetic devices.....None

Surgical or prophylactic devices.....None.

Possessions returned to Fade Street Police Station. Pending disposal ... all above.

Evidence value.....None

P.K.(HERBERT) LING, hawker of no fixed address. A hawker with a wristwatch that wasn't there.

Outside the wind was beating against the walls of the station as Typhoon Pandora, moving in fast, began reaching out with its swirling wall clouds for the Colony.

Trousers, fawn, tailored, socks, fawn, shoes, leather, brown... Whoever he was, for a hawker of no fixed address, Ling had had a certain degree of dress sense.

Feiffer looked down at his own creased suit and wondered if he were dead and stripped what someone might think of his dress sense. *Tailored.* If Ling had been wearing tailored trousers when he had been killed when his wristwatch and wallet had been taken by, no doubt, Staff Sergeant Shen and Superintendent Farmer and the rest of them, then he must have been wearing some sort of coat to go with it. Shirt.....1, tailed, silk, cream...

A silk shirt with tails that tucked into tailored trousers and no belt?

Everyone in Hong Kong who could afford a suit had it tailored.

P.K.(HERBERT) LING. Feiffer reached into the left hand pocket of his own trousers and, taking out his keys, pulled the pocket out and read on the little linen label

135

stitched into it: Kwong Man Se Tailor, 18 Cochrane Street, HK, phone 5-457205, Order No.98000891, and then, below that, carefully lettered in ink just in case of dispute, theft, or being left dead in an alley of Number 12, Hennesey Road near goddamned Fade Street: *H.J.Feiffer Esq.*

P.K.(HERBERT) LING.

Maybe they hadn't been quite as clever as they thought. Maybe they had thought that the possibility of anyone ever checking all their forms and notebooks and rubber stamps was as remote as...

...as meeting someone come as an emissary from the other world with hard, glittering eyes and death that moved in whispers.

Outside, the wind and the rain was hammering at the walls and windows as Feiffer, thirty yards inside the gates of Hell itself, moved quickly to the pigeon-holed Property shelves under the charge room desk and finding the neatly parcelled property he wanted, began looking for the label of a tailor who, like his own, wrote in the customer's name neatly in his best writing on the label, inconspicuously, at no extra charge.

*

Half way up the stairs to the fortune teller's room, Spencer seeing Auden's hand move towards his coat and the magnum in the shoulder holster under his armpit said quickly, 'Look, it's a mistake,' He began to move his hand to his coat pocket for his warrant card but, like Auden, found himself discouraged by a sharp jab in his back of the huge gun, 'Listen, we're the police.'

Mak the fortune teller, jabbing again with the shotgun, said in English, 'Yes.'

The fortune teller's room was full of people, what looked like the entire commercial population of Fade Street.

136

Mak moving into the room and taking a place between the group where he could point the shotgun squarely said, 'I know. And that's exactly why I'm going to kill you both and dispose of your bodies in the harbour during the typhoon.'

He glanced back at the group of people around him in the room – no less than fifteen or twenty of them – and, seeing them nod, knew he had their concurrence.

The safety catch on the shotgun made a clicking sound as he slipped it forward with his thumb to the *Fire* position.

*

In the cemetery on the edge of the waterfront, the rain and wind had combined into a single howling maëlstrom. Across Aberdeen Road the ocean surges had begun and water and spray was crashing over onto the road in a succession of heaving swells that sent boats and sampans bobbing and yawing with the force. By P.C. Tong, grass and earth around the recently dug grave was flying up into his face and onto his sodden clothing. He turned to O'Yee with his mouth wide open, his face streaming water, shouting, and no sound came out.

O'Yee heard him say, 'Eason! We thought Farmer had moved Eason!' He was wild-eyed staring at the rifle, 'We thought ... Koh and I, that...'

O'Yee trying to move forward, was held where he was by the force of the wind. The rifle was swaying in his hands. He gripped it hard and brought the muzzle up and held it with effort on Tong's chest. O'Yee shouted, 'The revolver ... take the revolver out and—'

Tong screamed at the top of his voice to be heard, *'We thought The Umbrella Man saw Eason being taken out of the station!'* The piece of paper with the three characters on it was flapping in his hand. He seemed to be trying to offer it to O'Yee to explain. Tong shouted, 'We saw him! Koh and

137

I—we saw him run and we heard the screaming and we thought—' The wind whipped at his hair and he turned his face away.

O'Yee shouted, 'Koh's dead!' He heard a sound somewhere behind him in the chaos – a car engine – and then it was gone again. His raincoat was flapping hard against his body like a drag rider in the tail of a stampede. O'Yee shouted, 'Where's Sergeant Shen?'

'We ran! Shen saw us run!' P.C. Tong tried to raise his hands up in desperate appeal. Water was running down his face and cascading off his clothing. Tong shouted, 'It was all Shen and Farmer and Koh, they were the ones! They liked it! They liked hurting people!' The notebook page was being wrenched out of his fingers by the wind. He held it up like a priest showing it to the gods, 'This is his real name! Now he can rest with his ancestors! It wasn't anything to do with me! What could I do? Farmer would have killed me too?'

'What the hell are you talking about?'

Tong said, 'The grave!' He turned and stabbed his finger at it, '*Ling!* Look at it!'

'I don't see anything!'

'They've given him his name!'

'Who has?'

'Them! *Him!*' Tong shouted, 'They know! They sent the man from the other world because this time we'd gone too far! We tortured his soul! It's all in the notebooks! Koh wrote them all out again but it was all a lie! They knew! They knew in the spirit world and they sent Death to us!'

O'Yee had no idea what the man was raving about. He looked around quickly and saw only a curtain of thick grey on the road. There was a light flashing somewhere – a marker buoy or something – O'Yee shouted, 'You know who I am! I want you to get rid of your revolver and then—' A blast of wind took him side on and he staggered

138

with the rifle being forced down. He saw Tong hesitate, 'I'll shoot if you move!'

There was a ramp a little way from the grave, for the undertakers' hearses and the processions. For a moment O'Yee thought he heard an engine there. There was a flash as if someone turned on a light. O'Yee, moving forward, said, 'Don't move! Just don't move!' The grave looked all right to him. If it had been disturbed...

Tong shouted, 'They've given him back his name! Can't you see? They've left the old characters for the name – for the name we invented – and they've—' He raised up the little piece of paper, 'I'm one of his murderers! *I'm trying to make it right!*' The wind caught him full blast in the chest and he staggered. Tong said, 'I've worked it out! I know who it is—!' There was a crash as something near the undertakers' ramp gave way and he turned to see it, seemed to collapse before O'Yee's eyes, and mouthed, 'Oh, no...!' He turned back, his mouth still open, looking for somewhere to run.

O'Yee shouted, 'No! Stand still!' He looked and saw only greyness. There was another crash through the storm and O'Yee turned back with the rifle and saw...

The bullets were going wide. In the wind, the bullets were going way off. On his knees, holding onto a gravestone for support, Staff Sergeant Shen fought with the weight of his revolver to keep it upright. There was a puff of smoke from the barrel whipped away instantly by the wind and then a howling sound as the bullet struck the ground by O'Yee's feet and whined off into the chaos. O'Yee shouted, 'No!' He saw Shen raise up the gun with difficulty. Tong was shouting something. O'Yee saw Tong a moment before he began to move. O'Yee said aloud, 'No, not again—!' He called to Tong, 'No, don't run!' He saw Staff Sergeant Shen look back suddenly, the gun waving wildly in his hand. He saw Tong running. O'Yee shouted out, 'No, don't run!' He got the rifle up and swung it against the wind towards Shen. He saw something moving behind Shen: a shape, a shadow, a light, sound coming through the wind in snatches.

Shen was turning, grasping the gun in both hands, falling. The shadow was almost on top of him. O'Yee saw him roll away onto his knees, then tense to get up and run. O'Yee was fighting the wind to get the rifle up. It was all happening for no reason, as if it was the wind moving Shen. *Tong:* where was Tong? O'Yee glanced back into the greyness and saw the man running. Shen was up and turning, moving away from Tong's direction: there was something behind him, coming closer.

There was nothing there!

He saw Shen's face, white with fear. The man was running, falling, through the graveyard. Lights were coming, growing brighter. O'Yee, losing his balance in the increasing storm, tried to bring the rifle to bear. *The damned thing was too heavy and awkward!* He saw... He saw...

The van, racing through the storm onto the undertakers' ramp suddenly seemed caught by a massive blast of wind and the last thing O'Yee remembered before it suddenly seemed to take wing and mowed him down like chaff against the disturbed grave was that it was all right, that the driver seemed to be wearing glittering airman's goggles and that all the passengers were therefore in good hands.

Mountainmen died hard. In the wilderness of rain and wind and gravestones O'Yee tried to force himself up, then, everything about it seeming only too simple and easy, he gave up and fell full length down onto the sodden ground and, without disturbance, thought he drifted quietly away.

*

It would have been just too easy by half. The label inside the pocket of the trousers read D'Arcy et Frères, Lusaka, in goddamned – of all places – *Zambia.*

140

In Zambia, evidently, those well known local African tailors, D'Arcy et Frères had never heard of hand-lettering customers' names on labels.

P.K.(HERBERT) LING ... whatever he was, he was no hawker of no fixed address.

The shoes and the rest of the clothes in the parcel were caked hard with blood.

Setting them out in a line on the cleared surface of the moisture glistening charge room desk with the locked and sealed main doors of the station in front of him banging hard and malevolently with the growing force of the wind outside, Feiffer began examining them closely, one by one.

11

In Yellowthread Street Constable Yan in temporary charge of the station, squinted hard at the telex message brought over from Headquarters by a partially drowned messenger and, wondering if his Grade One English qualification was all it was cracked up to be, scratched his head to make sense of it all and work out some of the words.

'Zim ... ba. Sel... ous. Zim ... ba. Do ... uwe ... Zim...' Picking up the phone to ring Fade Street he said the difficult syllables again, decided they sounded about as English as ... as nothing at all, and said in Cantonese exasperation, 'Aii-ya!'

'Zim ... ba...we...' The phone at the end of its dial tone made a clicking sound and he said carefully, still mentally rehearsing the words, 'Mr Feiffer, this is Constable Yan at Yellowthread Street.'

No reply. There was another noise and then, easily, unemotionally, and in a totally matter-of-fact voice, a recording began telling him that Typhoon Pandora in a move totally unforeseen by the weathermen, had reached Hong Kong early and the final warning signal in the meterological armoury, Number Ten, was at this minute being hoisted in the first probing fingers of what looked like being the typhoon of the century.

The Telephone Company message, covering all paid-up subscribers in the Colony, was on every line he tried.

The Telephone Company Warning Service would take,

from past experience, at least a full three quarters of an hour to release the lines.

Still peering hard at the message Yan heard the wind and the rain outside reaching breaking pitch and forced himself to go unhurriedly into the Detectives' Room to search the place for an English-Cantonese dictionary to translate the message into something that made sense.

*

In the fortune teller's room on Fade Street the gun was as steady as a rock. Mak the fortune teller said with a curious look on his face above the twin barrels of the gun, 'They paraded us all in to see the body. All of us.' He was speaking Cantonese so they could all understand and he jerked his head behind him to the assembled shopkeepers and merchants, 'One night at about midnight they came in with their uniforms all dishevelled and they dragged us out of our beds and paraded us all in the long corridor at the rear of the station and then, one by one, they took us down into the old air raid shelter and showed us what they had done.' He saw Auden begin to make the faintest movement of his hand towards the gun under his coat, 'All of us! We're in this all together—all of us!' If the message wasn't quite clear he stepped forward a pace and laid the barrels of the gun briefly on Auden's chest and glanced at Spencer to make sure he understood too. 'Nothing that happens in this room is ever going to be spoken of by any of us because we're all in it together.' He stepped back a pace and said for the benefit of his nodding colleagues, 'We discussed it. We thought we might be able to reason with you, but we can't.' He glanced around briefly at one of the shopkeepers, a slight nervous looking man twisting his hands together in front of him and shook his head, 'You're cops. What good would it do?'

The nervous looking man said in a soft, sad voice,

143

'You're all too clever for us, like the cat and the butterfly. You're all just too clever for us.'

Mak nodded.

Spencer running his tongue across his lips and nudging his side with his elbow to check his own revolver was in place asked, 'What had they done?'

'You know what they'd done! You were in it too!' Mak, his face twisting with sudden violence, said, 'You're all in it, all of you! You're the ones who are going to take over from them! For all we know you were the ones who put them up to it in the first place and took the money!'

'What money?' Auden, trying the rubber hose pose, said warningly, 'Now listen here, Mak or whatever your name is—'

Mak said, 'My name is Mak! I've left letters with relatives – not here, but somewhere else, somewhere safe – with my name written on it and no one, *no one* is going to take my name away from me! My name is *Mak!*' He nodded at the gun once, 'And that's why you're both going to die.'

Auden said, 'I haven't got the faintest idea what you're drivelling about! All this is a load of bloody crap! If you bastards killed all those cops then just come out with it and get on with whatever you think you're going to do!' He took a step to one side and caught Spencer's eye, 'But by God, you'd better hope that the pattern from the first shot catches both of us because if it doesn't you're going to see a fast draw in this place that'll make fucking Billy The Kid look like—' He saw something move behind a knot of the shopkeepers: another gun barrel pointed directly at his face and he said, suddenly deflated, 'Oh my God...'

Spencer, after a moment, said in careful Cantonese, 'We're not taking over Fade Street. We're from Yellowthread Street. Fade Street station probably won't be re-opened. It was a leftover from a redistribution of precincts or something and now that all this has happened—' He

144

saw Mak hesitate for a moment, 'If you people were killers you would have done it by now.' Spencer said, 'We're on your side. Tell us what happened.'

'You know what happened!'

Spencer said, 'No, all we know is that someone killed everyone in the station except for P.C. Tong and Sergeant Shen and P.C. Koh and that whoever it was trailed Koh to Yellowthread Street and—'

'*You* killed Koh in Yellowthread Street!'

Spencer said quietly, 'No.' He tried something, 'This isn't on the news or in the newspapers but Inspector Eason was working for Internal Affairs trying to convict the people at Fade Street of corruption.'

Someone in the back of the group said with heavy irony, 'Yeah.'

'Yes! And he was killed himself, not by the man with the bow, but by—'

Mak said easily, 'By Superintendent George Farmer with his service revolver, with one shot into the centre of the chest.'

Auden said in an undertone, 'Shit, Bill—' His hand moved towards his coat and finding the button that separated him from access to his gun, slipped it open between his outstretched fingers.

Spencer said, 'How did you know that?'

'Because we were there!' Mak said strangely, 'Don't you understand? They took one of us into the station that night and then they beat him to death. Shen, he was the one who did it! He was always the one. And then where normal men might have been frightened by what they'd done they just didn't care and they paraded us all down to see the body and the blood, and then when Inspector Eason came in unexpectedly the Superintendent – the top man himself – he just casually turned around and shot him dead.' Mak said, 'Bang! Just like that. Like a cockroach, like a nothing, and then...' The words failed to come out for a second, 'And then they just casually informed us that they could get rid of Eason so easily that they were even going to leave him buried in the station and that if we ever complained or told anyone—' The gun was trembling in Mak's hands. He was the most dangerous type of all, a man who had no way out, 'We have to protect our families from any more of it!'

Spencer said urgently, 'We're not taking over Fade Street. We're trying to find out what happened in Fade Street and bring whoever did what was wrong to justice!' It sounded very lame.

Mak said, '*Justice? Justice* has already been done! Every one of the bastards is dead and justice has already been done!'

Auden said, 'Oh, yeah, by who? By you? Is that what you think you're playing at now? A little bit of justice? You kill two cops in here and the only justice you're going to get—'

Mak's hand was touching obsessionally at the triggers of the gun, touching, squeezing, then relaxing on them, then touching at them again like a man trying to work out enough courage or hatred to shoot. Mak said, 'They buried that man without a name! They even tormented him after he was dead! They had all the forms, everything – all the doctors and the reports and the Courts and the undertakers – everything – *because they were cops* and there wasn't anything a decent man could do about it *except* kill them!'

Spencer said, 'Who? Who killed them?'

The nervous man behind Mak said quietly, 'I don't like this talking…'

Mak said desperately, '*All we wanted was to be left in peace!*'

Spencer said, 'The man who sold the future, was it him? Was he the one?'

'*They killed his brother!* They killed him in the air raid shelter! Shen beat him and beat him until he was dead!' Mak, lowering the gun slightly, said on the edge of tears,

'They beat him until he was dead and then when Eason came in – the one decent man in the place – they just killed him like a cockroach and kicked him to one side – like nothing more than—'

Spencer said, 'We know Farmer killed Eason. He hasn't got away with it.'

'Only because Farmer is dead! If Farmer hadn't been killed along with the rest of them you never would have found out – *ever!*'

Spencer said, 'Yes, we would.'

'Do you actually believe that?'

Spencer said, 'Yes, I do.' He looked at Auden, 'We would have found out, Phil, wouldn't we?'

Auden was silent.

'Phil?'

Auden said, 'Maybe.'

Mak said, 'You see! Even your colleague—'

Auden said quietly, 'I'm not like him, I'm like you people. He grew up believing that everything would turn out all right because that was the way the world was, but me, I grew up believing that people were out to get you and because they had more than you did, that was what would happen: that they'd get you. Unless you did something about it.'

The nervous man behind Mak said, 'Do you take bribes?' It was not an offer.

Auden said, shaking his head, 'No, I don't. Because no bastard on this earth is going to have anything to hold over me.' He nodded at Spencer, 'And he doesn't either because he thinks it isn't honourable.' He saw Mak's gun move imperceptibly from him to Spencer, 'But whatever happens I'm with him so don't think you can buy me off and lay a finger on him because if you do—' Auden said warningly, 'I'm not protecting Farmer and the rest of them because I've heard about them from all sorts of people and I know what sort of bastards they were, but if you pull the trigger on my friend here,' – he saw the snout of the other gun – 'Either of you…'

Mak said, 'We thought the business on the radio about the cat and the butterfly – the things The Umbrella Man saw – we thought they were all made up to frighten us even more!' He saw Auden and Spencer look blank, 'The cat swallowing a butterfly is a symbol in Chinese mythology for a long life being cut short.'

Auden said, 'Who the hell do you think killed all those people in the station—*us*?'

'Whoever wanted to take over their territory!' Mak said, 'They took thousands a week from us in bribes—thousands!'

Spencer said, 'And they used a lot of it to set up Eason just in case he got evidence against them.' He looked strangely at Auden, 'Maybe you're right, Phil, maybe I just don't know about real working people—'

Auden said, 'You do all right.'

The gun was lowering. Mak said curiously, 'But the only other person would be the brother of the man they killed and buried with the wrong name, but it couldn't be him because—'

Auden said, 'The man who sold the future.' It suddenly became clear to him. Auden said, 'I know people like you. You started off with nothing but ambition and then you found a man who went bond for you, didn't you? Someone who believed in you?'

Mak said, 'Yes.'

'And what did he do? Advance you money?' Auden said, 'Was he a man just like you who started off with nothing and who believed in all your businesses and advanced you—'

Spencer said quietly, 'The man who sold the future.' He thought for a moment of good men like Carnegie and Rockefeller and—

Auden said, *'And what the fuck did he charge you for that?'*

148

Mak said, 'A lot. But he—'

Auden said, 'How long ago did he start?'

'When we came. Two years ago, when they were going to tear Fade Street down and all the old tenants sold up cheaply and he got the planning laws changed and he—'

'And where the hell did he get the money from?' Auden roared, 'You stupid bastards! He got it from the *cops!*'

Mak said, 'We're all illegals! We're all illegal immigrants from China! He was trying to help us! He got money and the planning laws changed and he got—'

'Then why the hell didn't he get you papers to stay in Hong Kong?'

'Well, he—' Mak said, 'Well, we asked, but he said that the cops—'

Spencer said in a whisper, 'My God, Phil, are things really like this for people like—'

Mak said, 'But he couldn't have killed them all.'

'You said it was his brother they beat to death.' Auden said, 'Why? Why did they do that?'

'Because—because his own business overseas had folded and he said he was going in with his brother.' Mak said, 'His brother wanted to put in money for an equal share. He was a good man who—'

Auden said, 'So was Eason. He was a good man too. Maybe he was like me and my friend here. Maybe he just thought it wasn't right that life should be divided into classes and orders from the moment of birth. Maybe he just thought that every man should have the chance to make what he could of himself.'

The nervous man behind Mak said, 'That's why we came here—for that!'

Auden said, 'And they killed him and Eason and buried them both without even their names.'

Mak, on the edge of tears said, 'Yes!'

Auden, at the pinnacle of his argument, roared, *'And*

149

*what the hell if you're going to kill us and dispose of our bodies in
the typhoon are you people intending to do?'*

The nervous man behind Mak said curiously, 'Was it
really done with a bow and arrow?'

'Yes, it was really done with a bow and arrow!'

Mak lowered the gun. The second set of barrels in the
group disappeared from sight too. Mak said, 'I don't
think—I don't think we could have brought ourselves to—'
He was a beaten man. Mak said, 'We'll turn ourselves in
and you can send us back to China.'

Spencer said quietly, 'I didn't see any gun or hear any
threats, did you, Phil?'

Auden said, 'Are you kidding? With a fast draw like
mine?' Auden said firmly to Mak, 'Listen to me, there are a
hell of a lot of illegals in this Colony, but once you've made
it in you're in.' He paused for a moment, 'If you're fleeing
from China you can ask for political asylum.' He hesitated,
grimacing at Spencer, 'Anyone. All the people who swim
across or get across in worn-out boats: anyone. All you
have to do is ask for political asylum, and you can't be
sent back because it's against the charter of the United
Nations.'

Spencer said, 'I didn't know that.'

Auden said, 'No. Not many people do.'

Mak said quietly to Auden, 'Are you a Marxist, Mr
Policeman?'

Auden said, 'No, what I am is a fucking working man!'
He glanced quickly across at Spencer, the Phoenix Type,
and said with a shrug, 'Nothing personal.' He said quickly
and compellingly to Mak, 'Listen, give me the name of the
man who sold the future and we'll make a clean sweep of
every bastard in the place.'

Mak said, holding out to the last, 'They killed his
brother—'

Auden said, 'Yeah, and now he's killed them. So where
does that leave you? Better off? Or waiting around until

150

the next load of cops turns up to take over?' Auden said, 'If he came from China with you with nothing he found a ready made set-up in Fade Street falling to pieces. The cops couldn't take bribe money from people who had no money to give, so they set up your man who sold the future with a bit of future to sell and then, once you'd paid all that back – to them – they started taking your money in bribes to keep quiet about the fact that you shouldn't have been here in the first place. You don't honestly believe, do you, that the man who sold the future found his set-up money under a pile of rocks?'

Mak said, 'Were you happy in England, Mr Policeman?'

Auden said, 'I'm a damn sight happier here.' He said again, 'The name.' By God, he should have passed his Senior Inspector's exam! Auden said, 'The man who sold the future is also an expert on archery, am I right?'

Mak looked a little perturbed.

Spencer said, 'Right? He's right, isn't he?' He looked at Auden with admiration. A phrase from school about The Noble Savage crossed his mind, but he suppressed it quickly. Spencer said encouragingly, 'Right? Right?'

Mak said, 'No.' He paused for a moment, 'As a matter of fact, he's a cripple.' He looked at the nervous man, now wreathed in smiles. Mak said quickly, 'But he does have a bodyguard and maybe he—'

At the last trump, true to form, the Ox Type. Auden said, deflated, 'And his bodyguard, right, is a little old Chinese man with aristocratic connections who—'

Mak said, 'No. His bodyguard is a European who had business dealings with his brother in Africa before ivory exporting became illegal and he came here. By profession, I believe, in his own country, he was a soldier—'

*

He was too late. Everything in Fade Street had been

turned to nothing and he was too late. P. C. Tong, kneeling on the floor in the office of the man who sold the future looked at the figure in the wheelchair and had nothing left to do except place the little piece of notebook paper in the centre of the room, intone a chant over it, and, surrounding it with candles, make a prayer of atonement at the tiny family altar in the room.

P.C. Tong had his service revolver out, still attached to its white lanyard at his holster. He stood up and the gun banged against his side and followed him as he moved to the window and, hopelessly, watched the rain falling unstoppably down the pane and onto the street.

*

In Fade Street, Feiffer hung up the phone and looked at the carefully taken down spelled-out message from Yan. Moisture was glistening on the page and he picked up the handkerchief from the pile of bloody clothes, glanced at it to see it was clean, and used it to wipe the paper clear.

ADDIT INTERPOL MESSAGE REF IIA/967/CAA 1B 9HR UNSORTED INFORMATION YOUR OFFICE

NEW CROSSREFERENCE BRITISH COLONY RHODESIA

NEW CORRECTION INDEX READ 'ZIMBABWE'

HEADING: SELOUS SCOUTS

SILENT KILLING METHOD HAND HELD BOW REFERENCE FOUND WHITE OFFICER THAT UNIT

PREV. CRIM. REC: IVORY POACHING KENYA, UGANDA, ALLIED AREAS

NAME: CAPTAIN (ARMY RANK, RHODESIA) DOUWE ... REPEAT DOUWE NATIONALITY SOUTH AFRICAN

PRESENT WHEREABOUTS NOT KNOWN

MURDER LOOTING WANT WARRANT IN FORCE
ASIAN CONNECTION NOT KNOWN
LAST KNOWN ADDRESS CARE OF WING IVORY HOLDING COMPANY KENYA NOW IN VOLUNTARY LIQUIDATION
...DOES THIS ASSIST?
REPEAT INTERPOL MESSAGE REF 11/ACAA/1B 9H2 UNSORTED INFORMATION YOUR OFFICE...

The paper became moist again and Feiffer took up the handkerchief of the dead man and, unfolding it, opened it out to find a dry spot.

There was a single character embroidered in the corner of the silk handkerchief: a name.

The name, so close when written down in English in notebooks carefully recopied, so close as to be almost a mistake to be justified in the wildest eventuality of anyone ever finding out, was not Ling, but *Wing*.

It had been facing him all along. Through the running window of the station, blurred out in the rain, but there, directly across the road, there was a signboard proclaiming to the world that through a door not thirty feet away, should you suddenly need money to say, buy your way out of a torture chamber, *Wing And Company, Money Lenders*, would be happy to arrange it for you.

There was a sound in the corridor behind him, but Feiffer, staring at the sign with the handkerchief gripped hard in his hand, thought it was only the wind and did not turn around.

*

Mak said, 'Wing. The name of the man who sold the future is Wing. They killed his brother and buried him legally out in the New Hong Bay Cemetery under another name.' He saw Auden and Spencer writing it all down in their notebooks. He waited until they had got that part of it.

Mak said helpfully, 'Douwe, the name of Wing's body-guard is Douwe. I think he's a South African or something.' He paused for a moment, 'Before he was a soldier, I think he was a hunter.'

*

Camouflage clothing, that was what the cat thing had been. And the glittering eyes an old hunter's trick to keep a camouflaged hood on over the head—spectacles with the glass taken out and clear plastic put in so the eye holes would stay in position for the chase. O'Yee, covered in mud and slime, put his hand on the gravemarker and read the name of P. K. Ling and there, a little below it, where the rain had disturbed the grass, another pushed below ground level, another, the real one: *Wing.*

The Boys' Book Of Backyard Camping, Self Sufficiency For All, Wilderness Cookery, Pine Cone Pin, Campfires In The Canadian Rockies, Deer Skinning And Preparation For ... Modern Hunting Using Indian Secrets... O'Yee, pulling himself to his feet against the tombstone said, 'Bullshit! Bullshit! *Bullshit!'*

At the top of his voice, as the rain came howling in from the seawall, O'Yee shrieked in the direction of the whole stinking pile, 'You dirty, murdering, motherfucking, *son of a bitch!'* and reaching down for the rifle, got it into his hands and, limping and staggering, made his way across the graveyard towards the hunt.

*

In Fade Street, Feiffer said softly to Auden and Spencer, 'God Almighty...' He shook his head.

Spencer said softly, 'They were all in on it: the police,

154

this man Wing, maybe even at first, his brother. And then when the brother held back money or maybe changed his mind or wanted half the profits, they killed him.' He found it happened in minds he totally failed to comprehend, 'And then because he saw it happen, Eason.' He paused shrugging, 'Maybe Wing knew he was next. Or maybe it was just too much knowing that his brother was buried under another name.' Spencer said, 'And then they thought we were in on it too—all the cops, everybody.'

Auden said encouragingly to Feiffer, 'You can understand that, Harry, can't you?'

Feiffer nodded.

Spencer said, 'Maybe Wing wanted them out of the way so he could have the field clear to set up with another gang of cops that *he* could run instead of the other way around. Maybe he—' He said hopelessly to Auden, 'I never believed people could be so vicious to each other.'

Feiffer, still holding the handkerchief, said softly, 'Yeah. I know the feeling.' Feiffer said, 'It's gone quiet...' He paused and realised he could hear the station clock ticking.

3.10 p.m. In Fade Street there was a long hushed silence and then, as Feiffer and Auden and Spencer got out and ran for Wing's across the street, all at once, having come across hundreds of miles of ocean to do just that, with full force, Typhoon Pandora hit.

12

In the ceilings the ventilators were howling as they fought
off the rising pressure inside the room. Residual glass in the
boarded-up file room window was smashing and tinkling as
the rain and wind drove against it. There was a roaring
sound as everything in the room swirled upwards and then
a crash as the two empty filing cabinets crashed into each
other. Shen's hand was shooting waves of pain up and
down his entire arm. He let it fall down by his side and
blood came out from under his coat like the flow from an
opened tap.

In the Fade Street charge room, Shen got across to one of
the windows. It was straining and bulging with the
pressure. Rain was raging up and down the street in a solid
grey mass. He could see signboards and pipes and pieces of
scaffolding in it, banging and ricochetting off the road and
sending up spumes of water as they hit. There was a car
parked about fifty feet down from Wing's, bouncing and
sliding on its suspension. Feiffer and Spencer and Auden
were directly across from him, sheltering in Wing's doorway. Shen could see the plate glass window of the
establishment pulsing with the air pressure, running with
streams of water. Feiffer and Spencer had their heads down
in the doorway, crammed in hard against Auden. He had
missed walking in on Feiffer by a second and then, when
Auden and Spencer had come, he had been in the bushes
near the file room window when the typhoon hit.

His hand, shot through by a .22 bullet, was throbbing and when he grabbed at it with his other hand he thought he was going to pass out with the pain.

But he was O.K. He knew he was O.K. A sheet of corrugated iron from somewhere struck the front door of the station and careered off past the window, the sharp tip of it missing the glass by inches. The typhoon bar on the window was groaning and creaking with the effort of holding the glass together. Shen, dripping blood, got across to the charge room desk and hung onto it for support. The air inside the station was becoming explosively close and he had to force himself to fill his lungs and breathe out normally. There was a tinkling sound as one of the ventilators packed up on the ceiling and then a shower of plaster dust as the typhoon outside ripped the appliance loose from its fixings and half pulled it out through the roof.

But he was all right. Up on the hills and in the harbour the typhoon would be tearing squatters' shacks and boats to pieces and there would be landslips as undermined hills and redevelopment areas gave way and there would be dead and maimed and the homeless. The bullet had gone right through. He was not going to die from it and he would be all right.

The door to the squad room flew open in the roaring and he heard a tearing sound as a line of tiles was ripped off the roof like a zip fastener being wrenched open. In the space between the ceiling and the roof there were thumps as the insulation and wiring ripped loose and flew about in the confined space and then a wrenching noise as another ventilator, in chaos, stopped, jammed, and was instantly ripped loose.

He was O.K. He was still alive and no one would think to look for him in the station and when the typhoon was gone he could assume dead men's shoes and be gone.

Gripping his hand Shen nodded to himself and shouted,

'Yes!' There would be dead everywhere. He could take identification and join the queues of anxious and distraught getting out on the ferries to check the lives and property of their families in Macao and no one would take a second glance at him.

Everyone would have been hurt in some way: his wounded arm would mean nothing.

The front door was banging like a pile driver. He saw the grain in the wood weaken and start to splinter. He got to the window again, afraid that at any moment it might blow in. Feiffer was in Wing's doorway shouting something at Auden. He saw Auden with a shotgun hammering on the door. The car fifty feet away gave a lurch as the handbrake failed and skidded through the foot deep water in the middle of the road and careered crazily out of sight. Bamboo scaffolding and bits and pieces of metal and cardboard were flying in the air, spinning and whirling. Fade Street station was throbbing like his hand, groaning, giving way. He heard more tiles go from the roof and perspiration streamed down his face as yet another of the ventilators seized and the air pressure in the room rose and thrummed with heat.

He had almost walked in on Feiffer. He was O.K. He had luck. And the .22 from Wing's little gun had gone right through. Reaching into his pocket Shen got out a handkerchief and bound it around the wound and pulled the knot tight with his teeth.

He still had his service revolver. He had used it at the cemetery, missed, but none of that mattered anymore.

The ferry terminals would be packed with people when the typhoon was done.

And he had his money in a bank in Macao.

America. That was the place to go, maybe somewhere like San Francisco or—

He saw Feiffer step out into the street for a moment, his coat whipping hard around him, and try to look up to the second floor of Wing's. The wind caught him and he fell, reaching out for Spencer, and dragged back into the doorway again a moment before something flat and dark scythed down the street in the wind, caught a street light pole waving like a palm tree and, deflected, crashed into a banging sign board above an apothecary's shop and exploded it into splinters. Spumes of white foam were appearing in the water in the street as if someone was shooting cannonballs into it, the foam instantly being torn away in the direction of the wind.

There was a terrible roaring sound and a giant gap appeared from nowhere in the charge room ceiling as if a giant had ripped open the roof of a doll's house to see what was inside. The built up air pressure went straight up towards the roof and took everything loose in the room with it in a spiral. Water was appearing on the walls, leaking into it like the ocean broaching a submarine.

The station, groaning, creaking, throbbing, was giving way.

Shen got to the steel door of the air raid shelter and tried to pull it open. It was tight with the thrumming pressure inside. One of the steel cabinets in the file room was caught by an undercurrent blast and took flight, bent and smashed against the boarded-up window, jamming it.

His hand was shooting needles of white hot pain up and down his arm. He felt his arm stiffening, going useless.

He felt the door give a little. The charge room desk in the next room, hundreds of pounds weight of it, was giving against the bolts and devices that held it to the floor—it was throbbing like a heartbeat, moving, trying to break loose to come after him.

Shen screamed, *'I'm going to be O.K.!'* In the hurricane of noise he failed to hear the sound of his own voice. The desk was moving, coming after him.

Then the air raid shelter door gave easily and he inserted his good hand behind it and pulled, got himself around the weight of the thing and as it clanged shut in a sudden explosion of air, feeling saved, half fell down the flight of stairs and landed staggering, in the centre of the lysol-smelling floor of the darkened room.

Puffing hard in relief, he sat down for a moment to get his breath. He was going to be O.K.

Outside, the typhoon was nothing but a steady roar behind solid, secure, windowless two foot thick walls.

He found himself chuckling breathlessly, grinning, laughing, not quite believing it.

He was going to be O.K.!

He got himself to his feet and with all the time and optimism in the world, worked out the direction of the light switch at the top of the stairs and, his good hand out to probe the way, started in its direction.

Before he reached it, without warning, the light in the impregnable escape-proof underground cell went on and, in an instant, the blood still dripping unstoppably from his hand and fingers onto the scoured stone floor, all his dreams and plans were turned to nothing.

13

In his car, O'Yee shouted above the maëlstrom of rain and wind at the top of his voice, 'By God, you planned all this and people are doing exactly what you want them to do!' A third of the way down Singapore Road the trails all ran out into crashing water and wind and the only way to Fade Street was up through the wilderness of falling buildings and the rapids of the Colorado River. O'Yee shouted, 'By God, if you're a hunter, this is for you, isn't it?' The archer, the hunter, had brought his hunt to its consummation and now the only way out was in through the killing ground he had chosen from the first. O'Yee's car bouncing on its suspension springs like some sort of covered wagon caught in a twister bucked hard, lost its traction on the foaming road, and, as the engine drowned and died, lifted up and began to pivot on its back wheels to turn over. The Remington was across O'Yee's knees. He grasped at it as the car, still turning, slid across towards the sidewalk, collided with an awning support and, snapping it in half, turned over in a hail of falling bamboo and plywood.

It was still sliding away, going backwards on its roof. O'Yee got the driver's door open and bracing his feet against something, pushed himself out with the rifle still in his hands like a cavalryman creeping up on an Indian camp through shallow marshes. The car gave another wrenching noise and floated off, was caught by yet another

161

gigantic blast of wind as O'Yee made it into the shelter of a doorway, then, the open door ripping loose, turned over again and took brief flight and crashed in a cascade of water into another awning.

The wood of the doorway was good, solid oak: some sort of nineteenth century portal no doubt salvaged from the demolition of a government office fifty years ago. O'Yee got his face against the grain and pressed hard against the door with his hands. Good, solid, safe shelter. He glanced out into the street, clenching the rifle in his hands, and saw a log jam of planks and building materials coming at him through the water.

Bits and pieces of the roofs of the buildings opposite were flying off as the suctional force on the lee side increased momentarily and the windward side was caught in a vacuum. The wind had changed to a northerly. O'Yee, realising fast that he was on the southern slopes of the street, got out and splashed through to the next doorway.

The wind changed again and he was clamped into the doorway by a solid fist of air pressure. Then it changed again and he moved.

Lee, windward, northerly, southerly. *The Boys' Book Of Backyard Camping.* He got into a doorway in an alley and looked fast down its length and saw a gale of boiling, twisting grey air and dust and debris roaring at him. The most dangerous place to be in the mountains in a storm was under a tree with heavy branches. He glanced upwards, but the door had a solid steel girder lintel and he was safe. He drew in a deep breath as the twister came by sucking at the air in his lungs and then it was gone into Singapore Road in a rage of boiling white water flurries and banging window shutters and he was still safe.

Patience, foresight, planning. The hunter had to have unlimited patience and planning. That was why he had been at the cemetery in his van, waiting. He *knew* Shen and Tong would come there. Waterholes. Something crashed

162

into the flowing river of the alley with a whipping burst of white foam and O'Yee knew that the archer – the hunter, the predator, whatever he was – had staked out all the waterholes for his game and he was still waiting somewhere, still planning, still working it out. He was in his element. He was still...

At the cemetery— He could have killed either Shen or Tong easily at the cemetery but instead he had gone for O'Yee. A length of metal pipe, torn from somewhere, crashed into his doorway and span off, missing him by fractions and O'Yee shouted aloud, the words nothing in the chaos, 'Think! Think! Why not them? Why try to kill me?'

In the wilderness, if a hunter of his ability had tried to kill you then you would have been dead. Instead, he had driven the van hard almost in between him and Tong and then, judging by the tyre marks he had simply reversed out of there and gone back onto the road again. The tyre marks had not even been deep or uneven. The hunter, after he had removed O'Yee from the proceedings, had not even been in any hurry to chase either Shen or Tong because he—

Waterholes, oak trees ... The archer knew where his quarry was going to go to ground and he was simply leading them there a step at a time in order to get the best killing shot in possible. *The mark of the successful hunter is to know intimately the habits of his game.*

Why use a bow and arrow when modern science put everything at your disposal from goddamned automatic weapons to The Secrets Of Commando Piano Wire Strangling freely available in any bookshop? Lunatics and murderers were well catered for. It was all a game, a sport. He had worked it all out from the start and he was— He had made a mistake not getting his full limit at Fade Street, but, unperturbed, he had simply set out to track them down through the forest of buildings and roads and—

163

It made no difference to him that he was hunting in a city. He had probably broken up the street map into grids and marked buildings and houses and streets as if they were rivers and waterholes and game trails. In his safe spot, O'Yee, shaking his head, said, 'By God, as far as he's concerned, all we represent are the bloody natives! He didn't bother to get out of the car to check I was dead because as far as he was concerned I was just some savage who happened to get in his way on his trek to the killing ground!' Maybe it was even considered a point of dishonour to bag an animal you didn't plan to get. The wind changed direction again – he felt the northerly in his face – and he ran splashing through the briefly still water into Singapore Road and got into another doorway.

His car was gone, blown away out of sight into the greyness in the midst of a collapsed building at the end of the street. The wind changed again and he flattened himself hard back in the doorway for shelter.

Somewhere there was a final rendezvous. O'Yee said, 'Where? Where?'

Patience. Planning. Working it out in camp and then, unhurriedly, thoroughly...

The quarry. Think of the quarry.

A picture from one of his books flashed into O'Yee's mind: a book of game trophies and he saw the smug face of the hunter in the picture of the hunter sitting in his den below what looked like the stuffed head of the biggest antlered moose in the world. The caption had said something about the hunt taking ten days in which the hunter in the picture had passed up no less than half a dozen good-sized deer, an elk or two and no doubt three or four goddamned Alaskan Yetis solely in order to bring back the biggest—

Shen. The finest head to be had this day was Shen's.

O'Yee said, 'Where? Where?' If he was prepared to let

him go at the cemetery where did he expect to have him on his own terms for his trophy shot?

Where? Where?

The mark of the successful hunter is to know intimately the habits of his—

Where would Shen be driven to, find refuge, feel safe? There was nowhere safe in the Colony, all the doors and windows locked and bolted, all the public buildings by now taking lists of people they were sheltering and checking those names hard in the event of casualties.

Where? Where?

Somewhere safe, a known haunt, somewhere where the instinct of safety had been learnt over a long period of time, somewhere where the game felt free and unchallenged, where—

The man who had always delivered the money to Eason was Shen. Eason. According to IA, Eason had tried to ask Shen about the money but all he had got was an easy smile and—

O'Yee, suddenly aghast, said aloud, 'My God, according to Auden and Spencer that disused air raid shelter in Fade Street was *clean!'*

Someone, as it were, *lived* there. It was below ground, safe if he knew anything about second world war air raid shelters, behind two or three feet of windowless, blast proof metal strengthened with concrete and—

It was home. Even in a typhoon, it was the best clearing in the goddamned woods! And the archer knew about it because that was where he had dragged them all. And he had thought he was going to get all of them and lay them out on their own doorstep as a message that he had penetrated their last hiding place – that he was that good – that—

In every middle-aged American male there lurks a desire to get back to his— To his *lair.*

Fade Street.

That sonofabitch was waiting there for Shen as the dreadful magnetism of home and safety drew him closer and closer to it – *as the archer, the hunter had planned.*

Pine Cone Pin. The wind changed again and O'Yee, looking quickly from side to side for branches falling from trees or rivers swollen in the slopes and mountains that might slow up his progress, moved quickly and expertly through the wilderness of doorways towards the final game trail at the end of Singapore Road that led, inevitably and inexorably, to Fade Street.

14

In Fade Street everything in the street seemed suddenly to be in flight, the rain and wind raged against the sidewalks and gutters and coming off the steel window shutters of the shops and buildings like surf. In the doorway of Wing's Feiffer shouted to Auden, 'Shoot it off! Get your shotgun up against the lock and shoot the door open!' He saw Auden hesitate as a neon shop sign coming from nowhere careered into the sidewalk three feet away and exploded in a shower of coloured glass. A tangle of bamboo scaffolding was a little behind the sign: it struck the roadway hard in a spray of water and ricochetted off into the air.

Auden shouted back above the chaos, 'I can't!' He had the double-oh buckshot loaded riot gun from his car grasped hard in both hands and he was trying to keep it from being wrenched out into the street by the wind, 'If I shoot the door open the air pressure will blow in all the windows!' Tiles and bits and pieces of roofing material were being torn off the buildings on the other side of the street and taking to the air like flights of razor-winged birds. Auden shouted, 'There's only a typhoon bar on the plate glass window—' Something spinning crashed into the sidewalk and whined past him like a bullet, 'The whole of bloody Hong Kong is going! If we open that door—'

Spencer, yelling at the top of his lungs, banged Feiffer in the small of the back to get his attention. 'What about the back door? Maybe there's a backdoor in a loading bay or something and we can—'

Feiffer yelled back, 'We can't get around! There isn't any shelter!' It was like standing on the flight deck of an aircraft carrier as the full complement of aircraft pushed their jetstreams up to full power and blasted them full length down the runway. 'We can't get around to the back! We have to go in here! If we can get through the front rooms to the back before the windows go we can get a door closed and form an airlock!' A sheet of corrugated iron from somewhere miles away in the squatters' settlements missed the doorway by a foot, its sharp edges cutting a wake through the water on the sidewalk before it twisted and shot upwards, still spinning. Feiffer shouted in Auden's ear, 'Shoot that goddamned lock off *and that's an order!*'

Auden yelled, 'You're the one who's been in more typhoons than me! If you say the window won't go straight away—'

Feiffer yelled, 'Shoot the lock off!' He stood back, flattening himself against the side window as Auden got the gun up to waist level, tipped the barrel up to one side of the Yale lock high up on the door and – in the chaos it sounded like a popgun – blasted the wood around the lock to splinters.

The door banged open and whacked hard against the door jamb, the hinges bending and giving way. Feiffer got inside after Spencer and yelled, 'Put your shoulder to it to close it and we can keep the vacuum!' The door slammed closed, groaned hard under the sudden surge of pressure, then, as Feiffer glanced around quickly in the darkened room, bulged and began tearing itself to pieces as he held it. A length of wood ripped off down its full length. Around the blown off lockplate, the wood was coming off in long pared strips. Behind him, Feiffer could hear things in the room taking flight, banging and crashing as they hit walls and tables.

Feiffer saw a faint glimmer of light under a door at the

far end of the room and he yelled to Spencer, 'The door across the room! Make for the door!' He saw Auden turn around in the darkened room to test his glass theory by standing in direct line with the plate glass windows he was sure were going to explode into fragments and Feiffer, dragging him out of the way by the scruff of his neck, got over to the unlocked door at the same time as Spencer and slammed it closed after them.

There were bolts at the top and bottom of the door and, pushing with Spencer against the rising pressure in the front room, Feiffer got them shot into place. Auden was looking for something else to wedge the door with. There was nothing. In the front room on the other side of the door the windows exploded inwards with an earsplitting crash that turned all the glass in them to powder. Feiffer felt the bolted door bulge with the force and then shudder as something in the room lurched into flight and collided with it. Water washed in from the street was seeping under the doorway like acid. The door was bulging, giving way. Feiffer said, 'Come on! Come on!' reached the far end of the corridor, got the knob twisted open on the next door there and burst into the back room behind it.

The door to the parking bay at the rear of the premises must have been unlocked – it banged open with the change in pressure and then, mercifully, in a brief respite as the wind outside must have changed direction, slammed closed again. Spencer, moving fast across the room, got to it and shot the bolts hard to secure it.

There were candles everywhere on the floor of the room, all burned down and gutted, and the smell of incense around the outline of a man sitting in a chair.

Auden brought the riot gun up with a click, and then, in the same instant, dropped it again like a man accidentally swinging on a friend and said, *'Jesus—!'*

The chair had wheels on it and the man sitting there with one hand draped across his lap was not looking at him

169

at all, but up at the roof. Auden said, 'Christ, he's—' There was a solid, caked pool of blood on the floor all around the wheelchair and more blood on the chair itself and on the man's white shirt.

It was Wing, his gaping bloody throat cut from ear to ear. A door at the side of the room he had not even noticed opened and Auden brought the riot gun up again and shouted, 'Move and you're a dead man!' He saw a shadow standing in the door, dripping what he thought was more blood and he glanced at Feiffer and said awkwardly, 'It's—'

It was not blood, but water. P.C. Tong, standing in the open doorway to the side room, dripping rain from his drenched uniform, said softly in Cantonese to calm him, 'It's all right. It's just—' He saw Feiffer a little to one side with his hand on the butt of his still holstered gun and he gave the man an embarrassed shrug, 'I'm sorry about my appearance but you see' – tears were starting in his eyes – 'but, you see, I've been out in the rain for a long time and I—' His service revolver was resting on the floor at the end of his lanyard and he looked down at it and began hauling it up to put it away neatly, 'And I—'

Feiffer said, 'Don't touch the gun!'

'I've been out in the rain for a long time and I—' P.C. Tong said slowly, 'No, I—' He looked down at the weapon at the end of the lanyard and comprehended slowly, 'No, I—' He had something in his hand, out of sight, and he moved it slowly over towards the lanyard and pushed it against it and the weapon, released like a broken pendulum, made a dull thud as it fell to the floor. The thing in his hand was an open straight razor. Tong held it out in his hand and then let it fall onto the floor by the gun. He looked at Wing in the wheelchair. He was burping slightly with fear. Tong said, 'That's Mr Wing, the brother of the man we—'

Auden's riot gun was still on the man. Feiffer said

briskly, 'Tong, kick the gun and the razor over here.' He glanced quickly at Wing, 'Kick them in the direction of the wheelchair.' Tong was burping hard with fear. Feiffer ordered him, 'Now! Do it now!' Behind him, in the little room, Feiffer could see a workbench with draw knives and wooden blanks on it: the archer's bow and arrow manufactory. Feiffer said, 'Move away from the doorway.'

'It wasn't me.'

Feiffer said, 'Move away from the doorway.' He saw Auden take a step forward and said quickly, 'No, don't approach him!' He ordered Tong for the third time, 'Stand away from the doorway.'

'*It wasn't me!*'

Spencer said, 'I'll get him, Harry. He doesn't know what he's—'

God only knew what there might be within reach in that room. Feiffer said, 'Stand still.' He raised his voice, 'Tong, this is an order from a superior officer—'

'*It wasn't me!*' The burping seemed to be rising, taking over Tong's entire body. Tong said desperately, 'It wasn't me!'

Feiffer said, 'We know. Just—'

'*It was Shen!*' Tong's hands went to the sides of his head to keep his brain from reaching the edge of hysteria, 'It was Shen! Wing was already dead when I got here! I worked it out – just like Koh must have done – and after the cemetery I came here to—' He stared at the dead man in the chair, 'I came here to beg his forgiveness!' He thrust his hand in the direction of the candles on the floor, 'I tried. I tried to make it all right with his brother in the next world, but he was already dead and I couldn't—' Shaking his head he began looking hard around the room like a dog shaking himself free of water and searching desperately for his master, 'I—they were both here before me, Shen and the—and the other one, Douwe—*I got here after it was too late!*' Tong's eyes stayed fixed on Wing. His voice became conversational, 'I would have killed Shen for him to make it right—to make peace with his brother, but I—' He said apologetically to Wing's dead eyes, 'But it wasn't my fault. I just wasn't clever enough and I was hiding all the time and trying to—' He was sobbing, 'I just kept running and running and running in the rain and I just wasn't clever enough to work it out.' He said to Wing, 'I thought it was Eason come back, that's what it was. Koh and I saw The Umbrella Man shrieking as he ran from the station and we thought it was Eason come back – that The Umbrella Man had seen him – that Farmer hadn't really killed him at all and he'd got out of the room and he—' Tong said abruptly, 'Shen was behind us in his car and he saw us and he—he fled too in his car and we thought he knew something – Koh and I – and then we separated and tried to find Shen to find out what to do and he—' His eyes searched the room, seeing nothing, 'It was all Shen and Farmer, they were the ones! Farmer got everyone in to see what he and Shen had done to Wing's brother because they were so proud of it and then he got Koh to rewrite his entire notebook so it would look as if he wasn't killed by us at all but by muggers – *and then he got him buried under the ground in someone else's name!*' It was, at the end, more than he could comprehend rationally, 'Shen was Chinese himself and he didn't even give a damn about the next world and the poor man's torment!'

There was something glittering on the floor near the pool of blood under the wheelchair. In the poor light Feiffer tried to make it out, glancing back quickly at Tong.

Tong said, 'I'm finished. I've been driven insane by—by the rain and the running and now, I'm all—' He gave Auden a sad smile.

Spencer taking a step forward said gently, 'It's all right...'

Tong stepped back, 'No.' He raised his hand in the air like a traffic policeman.

172

Feiffer said, 'Where's Shen now?'

Spencer, moving slowly across the room, looked at Auden and shook his head for him to lower the gun. Spencer said soothingly, 'Listen, Constable, everything's all right. You're safe now. All you have to do—'

A strange thin voice came out of Tong. He said quietly, shaking his head, 'No, it's too late now...' He looked at Feiffer, blinking, 'I wanted the money Fade Street gave me because I had a dream of being a farmer one day.' He changed to English, 'Farmer—that's funny, that was the Superintendent's name: Farmer...' His dreams were private things and he went back to Cantonese, 'I wanted to grow things out in the New Territories...'

There were spots of blood on the floor leading to the back door. The shiny thing on the ground glittered at Feiffer. Whoever had made the spots was wounded and had gone out the door. The glittering thing was a tiny brass .22 calibre shell case, ejected from some sort of semi automatic weapon. Feiffer said quickly, 'Tong, where's the—'

Tong's hand went to his face and covered his eyes. The movement made Auden look up. Tong screamed, 'In the name of pity, don't bury me under my name or I might meet the man we killed in the spirit world and suffer like this forever!' His other hand was going towards his pocket, 'In the name of pity, don't—'

Feiffer, moving forward quickly, yelled at Auden, 'There's a gun missing! Wing's gun is missing!' He saw Spencer hesitate a few feet from Tong and look around, blocking Auden's line of fire.

Tong shrieked, 'For the sake of my spirit, bury me at sea where my soul will be lost forever!' He had the thing in his pocket out: a tiny black automatic vest pocket pistol, a .22. His hand was still covering his eyes. Tong shouted, 'In the name of pity, I'm sorry! I'm really—I swear, I'm *sorry!!*'

The little gun, fired once before in the candle strewn

room that day, was already cocked and ready to shoot and all he had to do as he put it quickly to his head against his temple was press the trigger and, with only the dullest, muffled detonation, it killed him instantly where he stood.

There was hardly any convulsion in his body as he fell and he went to Hell or the next world or Limbo – no worse than the place he had come from – with his other hand still clamped across his eyes, afraid of what he might see in the next world, having seen all he could bear of this, hoping, in his very last thought for nothing less than total, unknowing, complete and utter annihilation.

*

At the top of the stone stairs in the underground room, Douwe, his bow held loosely in one hand with the arrow already nocked, said smiling, 'This is the way they must have seen you, Shen, aye? Standing at the top of the stairs looking down at them?' His body, clothed in waterproof camouflage clothing, was relaxed and loose, the expression on his face smug and unhurried. The smile broadened a little and he nodded, 'That's right, Shen, think about the pistol in your waistband. Have a good, long careful think about how fast you can get to it and how fast I can draw my bow before you do.' The voice, speaking in English, was something unattached to him: the grey eyes above the smile were silent, watching. Douwe said, 'I heard about you from my friend Mr Wing. You were always the one I wanted. Mr Wing was sorry I didn't get you with all the others the first time, but I wasn't. I've been waiting for this for some time.' He nodded encouragingly, the flat South African accent coming out baitingly softly, 'It's always a pity to take the best trophy of the hunt by accident. It means more if you have to work for it.' He saw Shen step back a pace and get a good balance on the balls of his feet. 'I see a lot these days how some people go on safari with

174

cameras or they track a beast until they've got it in rifle shot and then they shoot on an empty chamber.' He furrowed his brow to see if Shen understood what he was saying, 'But I don't go in for all that self-serving conservation stuff. When I track a beast or a man I want, I kill it.' He made a little shrug, 'You see, for all you know, if you had a live round in the breech of your empty gun the round could be defective or maybe the wind could take it or the animal might move – and you'd never know.' His bow hand was loose on the handle of the weapon, the silver flights on the barbed shaft glittering slightly against the dull khaki sleeve, 'No, I always kill what I track.' He looked down at the flagged stone floor. The smile had gone. 'My friend Mr Wing did me a service in Africa, by helping me get out. The one you killed. That Mr Wing. They're a bit like Africans, the Chinese, they never forget a wrong you do to them – and you shouldn't have put the poor bugger in the ground under another name because that just doesn't sit right.' The arrow hand was well away from the shaft. Shen, watching, tried to calculate how fast the archer could move if he… Douwe said, 'That was the first thing Mr Wing asked me to do: to put a second marker a little under the ground on the grave so his brother could rest in peace.'

There was a tic starting in Shen's face. He controlled it.

Shen said evenly, 'Wing's dead.'

'That's right.'

'I mean your goddamned cripple! I cut his goddamned throat!'

Douwe nodded. 'I thought you would. I could have saved him, but I wanted you. After the cops left I was in here, upstairs, watching. I saw you hiding in the bushes. And Tong, I saw him at the end of the street. He went into Wing's too, just after you'd left.'

'If he went in he knows all about you!'

Douwe shrugged again. 'No, he's at the end. He's like

Koh and Farmer and all the rest of them. Just a hyena, something you kill because it's a nuisance. He was useful as a tethered goat to get you, but I don't think he matters now, do you? There's plenty of time for him.'

'He'll matter if the cops get him! What the hell are you going to do then? Kill every cop in the world?'

'No.' Douwe drawing a breath, said, 'You're the top dog, Shen, that's why you came back here into your lair and not Tong or the other one Koh. Koh I killed running away into unfamiliar country and Tong, well, he doesn't count any more, but you—'

I've got a fortune stashed away! It's all yours!'

'For what?'

'What do you mean for what? *Money!'*

'I could have had Wing's anytime I wanted it.'

Shen's mouth went dry. In the little room he could hear the humming of the typhoon against the solid stone. The archer was watching him, savouring it. Shen's hand was throbbing with pain. The revolver was in his waistband. All he had to do...

Douwe said quietly, 'Do it. I'm going to let you do it, so any time you like...'

'What the hell did you do it all for? A *favour?* Because that crippled bastard's brother did you a goddamned *favour?* I'm offering you a fortune! Have you any idea how much there is? I've got Farmer's money and all the rest of them—it's all in Macao in numbered accounts and I know the numbers! I can give you enough money to—' He started his hand for the gun and then drew it back again, *'What the hell do you want from me?'*

The archer was smiling again. He said in an admiring voice, 'Yep, you really are first rate, and I find I really want what you've got very much indeed.'

'There isn't anything else! What else is there except money? I haven't got anything else! I've got a fortune and it's—*what the hell else have I got?'* Safaris, lairs, tracking...

176

Shen said suddenly, 'Oh, no...' His mouth went dry and he felt every nerve in his body paralysed. Shen said again, 'Oh, no, no...'

Douwe said, 'That's right, Shen, just like a prize animal I've tracked for a long time and outwitted on his own terrain' – his fingers curled around the arrow as he started to move the bow forward to put it into position for the draw, 'That's right, Shen—I want your fucking *head!*'

He said quietly and evenly, 'Time's run out. If you're going to try your luck getting to the gun, now's the moment to do it.'

15

In the howling gale in the open parking bay through Wing's back door, Feiffer shoved his way out of the rocking car parked behind the anonymous looking van and shouted out at the top of his voice to Auden and Spencer, 'There's blood on the seat and the thing's been hotwired! It's Shen's. He must have tried to start it and given up. There's blood all over the wires. It must have been a hand wound or something!' Auden was by the front of the van, pulling hard at the door against the pressure of the wind to keep it open. He had something in his hand, passed out by Spencer. Auden held it up so Feiffer could see it and mouthed, *'An arrow!'* He held the door open with both hands for Spencer to get out and then let it go with a crash. 'Harry, the engine of the van is cold. The archer must have left before Shen got here otherwise he would have killed him on the spot!' He looked up as the back door to Wing's flew open with the wind and then crashed shut again in a fountain of water, 'Tong must have been a little behind them and—'

Feiffer shouted, 'Where the hell are they now?' The rain increased suddenly and came down in whipping torrents. There was only one place safe within running distance, one place buried under the ground with walls two feet thick that... Grasping Auden by the lapels to steady himself as he slipped in the raging water Feiffer yelled, 'The station! They're both in Fade Street station across the road!' He staggered through the rain and wind, half dragging and being pulled by Auden and Spencer, 'We have to get across the street to the shelter before they—' He got the back door open and was greeted by a chaos of blasting wind and airborne papers and debris. Both the corridor doors had gone and he could see directly through out of the smashed window across the street to the station's driveway. The street was a raging torrent.

Auden shouted, 'Goddamned Blondin couldn't get across there now! It looks like goddamned Niagara Falls!' He got inside the door and tried to push it shut and called to Spencer, 'Give me a hand!'

Spencer staring hard in the direction of the burst in main door yelled, 'I can see someone! He's at the driveway going around to the rear door!'

Auden yelled in protest to Feiffer, 'I thought you said the goddamned glass wouldn't blow in!' He looked hurt as Feiffer, drawing his gun and disappearing into the corridor like a man swimming underwater through a whirlpool yelled at him to forget the back door. Auden shouted, 'You can't get across there! You'll be blown half way to fucking China!' Spencer was down the corridor after Feiffer. Auden shouted, 'What the hell do you think you're—' He saw something moving through the greyness across the road, a figure caked in mud, drenched to the skin, with something held hard in his hands against his body, someone limping slightly.

O'Yee. It was O'Yee and he was half way up the driveway heading towards the rear door of the station.

Auden yelled out in warning at the top of his lungs, 'It's goddamned O'Yee! He doesn't know they're—' He saw the riot gun lying in a pool of water by Wing's overturned wheelchair and let go of the door and got across to the room to get it as the door, caught in the sudden awful pressure of the typhoon reaching full, unfettered pitch, slammed once, then, bulging briefly like rubber, ripped off its hinges and burst into matchwood.

179

*

It was now or never.

Now or—

Shen said suddenly, 'You stupid, dumb, mindless, *savage!*' and thought, a moment before the arrow, moving in a blur of release across the room, skewered him through the heart and killed him where he stood, that he had actually got his hand around his gun and was drawing it from his waistband.

*

There was glass still flying from the smashed plate glass window, the typhoon bar broken loose and swinging from its mounting on the floor like a scythe. A section of glass still holding on ripped itself loose from its putty and exploded into fragments into the room, missing Feiffer's face by inches as he whipped his arm up to protect himself.

Spencer was at the burst open front door, being blown out. He got his arm around the jamb and pulled himself back in, was deluged in a torrent of rain as the wind changed direction and, slipping on the running floor, lost his balance and went sliding out again.

Feiffer was being pushed and pulled across the room by the force of the wind. Getting down onto his knees he sprawled full length behind the protection of the window's floor mounting, caught Spencer by the hand, saw Auden being propelled out of the corridor in a fusillade of flying debris and broken wood and shouted, 'Give me a hand!' He caught Spencer by the arm and wrenched him in.

The street was a river of foaming white water and flying metal and wood. A street sign advertising something caught a parked car and smashed out its windscreen then

180

the car, its balance gone, turned over and began sliding on its roof down the street.

Auden, getting under cover below the window frame, yelled, 'How the hell are we going to get across there?' A shower of glass from panes left in the broken open door imploded and banged into the rear wall of the shop like bullets, 'You said the window wouldn't go!' He saw the car across the road still sliding begin to rip apart, the doors going first, and yelled again, '*How?* How the hell are we going to get there?'

*

There was a final job left: the last payment to Wing, something he owed, and the archer did it expertly, without hesitation. The wind outside was thundering against the thick walls of the air raid shelter and, bending over Shen to carry out his task, the archer listened to it and made plans to get away on the lee side through the forest of doorways and awnings to Singapore Road.

He had a single arrow left, clamped onto the upper limb of his bow by two rubber half-circlet clips and he tested its edge and checked that it was secure.

The clipped back skinning and boning knife on the floor had done its job and he locked the blade and slipped the weapon back in his pocket. There was another object by it and he picked it up to take it away with him. He heard a sound from somewhere upstairs, but it was only the wind or the ventilators and he stood up with his bow in his hand, looked down once at Shen, and, moving on the balls of his feet, went up the stairs to make good his escape. He had put dry rubber overshoes on over his wet boots when he had come into the station so as not to make tracks and now, as he went, the overshoes made no sound.

Only Tong to go. He knew where he would be. The

route into Singapore Road would take the archer circuit-
ously, still on the lee side of the wind, directly to Wing's
back door.

He made it to the top of the stairs and got the door open
in the chaos of noise and vibration in the station and,
glancing quickly at the bulging, straining windows on
either side of the main door in the charge room, glanced
down once at Shen's dead body and, grinning to himself in
satisfaction, turned to make his way out.

There was something awful standing at the door of the
squad room, drenched to the skin and covered in mud and
filth like camouflage markings. It was the cop from the
cemetery. In his hands, held ready at hip level for a
quick-kill shot, he had a scoped Remington hunting rifle
and the eyes were steady, unblinking and decided.

O'Yee, the water dripping from his clothing in the dim,
deadly room, the chaos outside subsiding to a steady
humming in his ears, said with terrible unarguable promise
in his voice, 'Move, and I'll kill you where you stand.'

The archer's hands went to the arrow in the bow quiver on
the limbs and O'Yee, getting the rifle up higher, shouted, 'No, not twice! Leave it now or you're a dead man!'

*

In Wing's, the eye of the typhoon was never going to
come. In the teeth of the storm Feiffer shouted to Auden,
'It's no good, we can't wait!' He looked around desperately
for something to help him get across the road, but there
was nothing. To attempt the crossing as the swelling waters
backed up the drains and gutters and span in whirlpools
would be suicide. Bits and pieces were beginning to rip
away from the sides of the building and he could see a
flight of tiles from the station wrench themselves skywards
and spin up and then accelerate as the winds caught them.

The eye of the typhoon. *Where the hell was the eye?* The

182

windows in the station were still intact, bulging, thinning, fragile, about to burst into powder. He looked down at his snub-nosed revolver and knew it was hopeless.

Auden. Auden with his Colt Python loaded with his illegal, non-regulation, goddamned murderous .357 magnum round. Feiffer yelled, 'Phil! Your revolver! Give me your revolver!' There was one chance, the longest of long shots. If O'Yee was in there and in trouble, then...

He saw Auden hesitate.

Feiffer yelled in the chaos, *'Give me that fucking gun of yours!'* The wind was at its topmost peak. The eye could not be far behind, but there was not time.

Feiffer, grabbing the gun from Auden, took it hard in both hands and, bracing himself as best he could against the side jamb of the empty window frame held the kicking and bucking gun against the wrenching power of the wind and tried to get a bead on a window.

Spencer yelled, 'Harry, I'll try to make it across the road if you—' and Feiffer yelled at him, 'Shut up!' and his heart in his mouth, drew back the hammer on the giant long barrelled weapon and, waiting for the exact, steadiest moment, began squeezing the trigger.

*

O'Yee shouted, 'No!' He was paralysed with fear. Koh had taken the arrow through the back and it had ripped him apart and crashed against the wall with an explosion of plaster dust that had... Pine Cone goddamned Pin... The rifle was moving in O'Yee's hands, coming up, his thumb pushing hard at the safety catch as if it was broken, the firing pin in the bolt paused ready to leap towards the percussion cap on the cartridge...

It was a nightmare. He couldn't move.

The archer shouted, 'You've tracked me, man! So here's your fucking trophy!' and he was throwing something as, at

183

the same time, the arrow nock went into the string and the bow raised, was coming back.

'I cut it out, man, so he couldn't even make excuses in heaven!' It was all happening in slow motion. The bow was coming back. 'Wing's idea, man – no one like the Chinese for revenge!'

It was Shen's tongue. O'Yee said, 'Oh my God—!' and knew he shouldn't have taken his eyes off the bow to look. The bow was coming back, at the fullness of its arc. The archer seemed to be saying something, to be laughing at him. The archer shouted above the chaos, 'Time to die, man! Time to—'

O'Yee got the rifle up and knew he was pressing at the trigger, knew he was dead at the moment the arrow reached full draw and was released across the room, knew that...

In Wing's, Auden shouted, 'For God's sake, don't miss! It's the only magnum round in the gun!' and as Feiffer fired and the left hand side window in the place went and the building, its final tenuous hold on the ground gone, began tearing itself to bits before his eyes.

It had missed! The wind had caught it and it had missed! O'Yee saw the arrow to one side of him smashing against the plaster work by the main door, glass showering in around it like smoke and he thought, 'My God, it's actually missed...'

The gun. He still had the Remington and— The room was falling apart, the entire roof going in a single monstrous tearing, the floor under his feet lifting up in planks and pared splinters of weakened wood. He felt his hair whipping against the side of his head as the blast from the typhoon seemed to be coming directly from the centre of the charge room and wrenching the walls and floor to pieces. The bow was gone: he saw it on the floor being spun around like a compass, all the arrows shot, and he thought, 'I've won! I've beaten him!'

He looked up and the archer was in front of him with his hunting knife out.

O'Yee shouted, 'I've—' and then, in the chaos of the exploding room the archer, still unbeaten, launched himself at him like a tiger.

16

The entire roof had gone and rain was pouring in from the smashed and fallen ceiling. The water tank had been broached in a tangle of pipes and connections and its contents cascaded down onto the floor and sluiced the entire length of the charge room like a tide. The first thrust had taken him through his rubber cape at the left bicep and water or blood ran back down his arm and onto his chest as O'Yee twisted to get out of the archer's grasp. Impossible to kill a man by a knife thrust directly to the heart – he had read that somewhere – the ribs got in the way, and the only known method was an upward driving blow at the diaphragm. He had read somewhere that the Malays said that in their tribal warfare days that the only way to stab a man to the heart was if he was lying on his back... O'Yee, full length on the ground, got his hand around the archer's knife wrist and pushed it back as hard as he could, his free hand feeling for the rifle. The rifle was gone and the man's arm had the strength of solid, unmovable steel.

Under him, the floor, weakened by Scientific's excavations, was going: he felt it giving way under his back. A flood of water washed over him and covered his face. Spluttering, still holding onto the knife hand, O'Yee twisted, suddenly relaxed his grip on the archer's hand, and the knife thumped down past him like a pile driver and imbedded itself into the floor.

The archer's face was an inch above his own. He saw the man's mouth drawn back over his teeth and the alarm in his eyes as the knife missed and he fell forward with it. It was like trying to fight a man under water. O'Yee felt something against his free hand and wrenched it up by its stock, ready to twist it and get the barrel into line to shoot. It was not the rifle at all, but a piece of plank. The archer was rolling back on top of him, the knife grinding in the planking of the floor as he tried to pull it free. O'Yee's hand seemed stuck on the plank. It was not a plank at all, but a section of the charge room desk – something heavy. He tried to get his hand around it to find purchase to bring the object up to swing it, but it was stuck fast. He tried to roll with the archer and break his hold, but the man got his free hand around O'Yee's throat and held on, going for the windpipe. He had read somewhere that if you got your fingers around a man's windpipe and squeezed, when your fingers met...

O'Yee felt the knife come out free from the floor and he bunched his fist and hit the man as hard as he could across the side of the head. It was like hitting a bowling ball. The archer made a grunting noise and the fingers, pausing only a second, went on squeezing.

The humming in the air turned into a buzzing and O'Yee felt his head swelling. The water sluiced over him and turned hot as the blood in his neck was cut off and he felt himself being suffocated. He got his fist back again and hit, but there was no force in it.

His revolver. It was still there under his coat, pressing against his armpit in its shoulder holster, an impossible, unmanoeuvrable distance away. The knife was coming up again: O'Yee felt himself losing his grip on the archer's wrist. The archer's face was disappearing in a blur. He saw the water cascading down from the ceiling and thought he was drowning under a waterfall in the mountains some-where, being pushed deeper and deeper into choking, thick mud. Glass was tinkling and falling in the room. He heard a howling from the wind and then a deep crash that seemed to come from somewhere in the small of his back as something heavy in the charge room was hurled across the room and collided with a wall. His hand contacted something or something fell on it. He felt it bounce and slide in the water: a brick. He got his hand around it as the knife came up and with his last effort before the blackness overtook him, drove it hard against the side of the archer's head. No force. Threre was no force in it and he was...

He felt the terrible pressure on his neck stop and sweet air flooded into his lungs and he had surfaced from under the waterfall and was breathing. The archer was gone. He felt the sudden release of the weight of his body. There was no buzzing. The sound was a solid, non stop roaring as the wind tore at the ceiling and took bits of it off and up like shrapnel and then there was a rending tear as one of the main joists wrenched itself loose and crashed into the foot deep water like a log going into a river.

He got to his feet and, the room in chaos, was knocked down again. The archer was gone. O'Yee saw the charge room desk lying on its side being picked up by the wind again and then, in the moment that it left the ground, another of the great wooden roof joists came down and pulverised its surface like plywood. The main door was bulging and shaking, about to go. He tried to get up and one of the side windows, hanging jagged glass, exploded inwards and showered him with mortar and wood fragments. His gun. He had to reach his gun. The rubber cape was twisted around him and, still breathing hard, even to break open one of the studs holding it was an effort. It may have taken seconds: it seemed... It seemed as if he was still lying on the floor trying to work at the studs, but he was up on his feet being pushed by the wind, moving towards the squad room. The archer was gone. In a daze, O'Yee turned and tried to go back into the charge room. Doors and cupboards were swinging open, banging and breaking up. He saw something in the corridor spin against a wall like a spear and break up – one of the brooms from the cupboard. The corridor was awash and part of the inner wall had come down, exposing the skeleton lattice work behind the linings. A blast of raging air hit him from somewhere and spun him around, still pulling at his cape, and O'Yee thought, 'He's gone. I've missed him. He's gone back into the mountains.' The world around him was still blurred, in metamorphosis, and he saw water come down from a smashed corner above the closed rear door of the corridor like a lava flow. The station was breaking up. He heard a deep, rending sound under his feet and the floor planks under the water split and opened up and he turned and fell back into the charge room to escape being dragged under. Like a man in a dream, O'Yee staggered, trying to undo the infernal, undo-able studs, feeling the weight of the gun under his armpit, nestling there, impossibly un-get-at-able, tantalisingly—

The archer was there, at the front door, pulling at the bolts, trying to get out. O'Yee got to him and caught him around the neck. The knife was gone: he saw both the man's hands snap open as he wrenched him back and then, losing his footing on the floor, slipped backwards and crashed back into the waterfall, still holding him.

The archer's head was under the full force of the water cascading down from the ceiling, his camouflage jacket filling up like a balloon and turned him into a dying fat man. The archer's hands were snapping open and closed and O'Yee, still holding on in the tidal surge, twisted at him and tried to get his face under the water. He saw something surface for a moment, floating, then half submerged again – the Remington – and O'Yee let go of the man's neck and reached out for it, but it had moved underwater and all he got was a handful of empty, useless water. He was going, fading: his strength had been sapped fast, his heart bulging in his chest and expanding, ready for the easy knife thrust through the unthrustable soft ribs.

The archer was on his feet, bracing himself to get a stance. The rifle was gone. O'Yee swung his leg as hard as he could through the water and connected with the archer's ankle or his boot and scythed him back down to the floor. He saw the varnished rifle stock bob up for a moment, water running from it as per the stockmaker's promise in unharmful droplets and O'Yee, on his hands and knees, made for it and caught it by the comb. It slipped away in his hands and sank again and he scrabbled down under the water for it through the submerged debris of falling pipes and fittings from the water tank.

He got it.

Then it was gone.

He saw the shadow of the archer behind him, getting up, looking around, and he touched something hard with his clasping hands and caught it fast: a pipe, some sort of plumbing. It was the rifle barrel. Too late he swung it hard like a baseball player going for a low one and knocking the archer to the floor, not by the blow but by the proximity of it, smashed the rifle stock uselessly to pieces against a shattered roof joist. The magazine went too. He saw an eruption of brass shells break up from the restraint of their magazine spring and fly across the room. They had all gone into the water. There was one live round in the breech. O'Yee pulled what was left of the rifle back from the joist and tried to turn it on the archer, but when he tried to get his finger through the trigger guard there was nothing but twisted, jammed, useless metal. A solid wall of water came in from somewhere – as part of a wall went in a bursting collapse of bricks and rubble – and O'Yee felt himself being overturned, grabbing and reaching out to stop himself being dragged under.

He was being swept away down a river, bits and pieces of wood and logs passing by him lethally close as he went over and over towards the waterfall. Something hit him against the side of the head: a rock or something on the surface, and then he was caught fast by a plank or half submerged obstacle and held fast, his rubber cape knotting and holding him, pulling him down.

The rear wall of the station went like a dam bursting and foaming water burst in sideways into his river and turned it into a whirlpool. He was being carried away. He saw a gaping darkness ahead, a cave, the water bursting over it and falling away and he thought, 'The falls!' His cape was ripping and at the same time holding him fast. He felt a long section of it give way and he scrabbled with his feet like a man falling from an airplane and found nothing solid to hold on to. Through the gaping roof rain was pouring down on him. He saw the greyness of the sky closing in, coming closer. Whatever was left of his cape began to give way and he swivelled around under water, pushing and grabbing to get his chest up as, in a single tearing sound that he thought came from his body suddenly giving way, he was picked up in the water and launched like a cork towards the terrible blackness of the cave passage where the white water was going.

The steel door to the air raid shelter was jammed open, water swirling around as if it was a rock sentinel marking the end of the trail, and O'Yee, his cape ripped from his shoulders and stuck around a broken sharp plank in the middle of the charge room like a sunken warning pennant, was swept through against the open door jamb and lodged there. The air raid shelter was a foot deep in swirling river, the drainage outlets in the corners of the room foaming as they began to back up with the debris and water and clog.

He saw Shen's body, floating, blood swilling around it like marker dye.

The archer was pulling at Shen's waistband, trying to lift him up. He had the butt of Shen's gun in his hands and, like a looting scene from Hell in the grey semi

191

darkened room, he was trying to pull it free from Shen's sodden, twisted clothing and cursing.

Outside, the wind from the typhoon, in a final complete blast, smashed in the main door of the station and sent it flying and, in an instant, the eye arrived and all the noise stopped.

He was over the edge.

The final surge of water caught him in the small of the back and something delivering him a terrific crack on the side of the head, O'Yee was washed unstoppably down the stairs and into the abyss.

*

Feiffer was still shouting. In the sudden total silence he yelled to Auden, 'It's the eye! We've got about half an hour!' He saw the police station clearly for the first time, 'Jesus Christ, there's nothing left!' The flow of the water lessened and he waded out and, still holding Auden's enormous gun, yelled at the top of his voice, 'Christopher! *Christopher!*'

*

He was panting, puffing, on his feet. O'Yee, his gun drawn and pointing directly at the archer's head, said at the end of his 'battered, bruised and bloody humanity, 'You dirty, lousy, stinking sonofabitching motherfucker, I'm going to put you down like a goddamned mad dog!' He felt the air coming in gasps through his flared nostrils. He was standing over the hunter, 'You dirty lousy bastard, I'm going to blow your fucking head out through your goddamned eyeballs and then I'm going to cut your heart out and feed it to the fucking vultures!' The gun in his hand was trembling. He got his other hand onto the butt and gripped it, 'I trailed you, you bastard, and I took you

192

on man to man and I may drop dead one day of a fucking heart attack, you murdering goddamned badlands bastard, but you, you I'm going to put a ball in and leave you dead on the trail like goddamned carrion meat for the fucking buzzards!' He was raving. His head, thumping like a bell, was spinning. O'Yee said, 'I want you, you sonofabitch. I want you for the goddamned scalp shelf in my tepee!' The gun was wavering in his hands. His feet apart, he anchored himself on the floor and tried to keep the man's face in focus, tried to shake his head to clear it and said, 'Christ, what's happening?' He was running down like an old clock, getting out of breath, reeling. He saw his enemy get to his feet and stand facing him and he shouted, 'Stand still, damn it! Don't make me shoot!' O'Yee, wanting to put his hands to his face, said vaguely, 'Count coup, want to—' The suddenly stilled air was ringing. O'Yee said— 'Want to—'

'Take it!'

There was a voice. O'Yee couldn't focus on it. The gun was wandering in his hand. He hardly knew what he had it out for. O'Yee said, 'What? Take what?' Someone was talking to him. O'Yee said, 'What? What did you say?' There was blood running down the side of his face and he let go of the gun with his left hand and put it up to his temple to make sure it was real. O'Yee said, 'What? Take what?'

He was hurt. The archer hadn't got up at all. He was still on the ground next to Shen under O'Yee's gun. And he was hurt. Something inside his chest seemed to be broken and he had his hand on it, pushing on it, the pain draining the colour from his face and registering in his eyes. The archer said, 'I'm like you, man, I'm a hunter—'

O'Yee, shaking his head, said, 'No, I'm a—'

'Take it, man! Take the trophy! The hunt's yours, *take it!*' The archer, pressing against his chest with his hand, got to his knees and reached out to Shen's body for support, 'The head! Take the goddamned *head!*' He saw O'Yee losing focus, the gun wandering, 'You're like me, aren't you? Africa's all finished. This is the last hunt. *Take the fucking head!'*

Emily could do the cooking of the ... of the dead game, of the fur bearing animals for trade – but if she cooked them how could he trade their fur...?

Of course, he could take the fur off first ... and Harry, he was the ideal sort of person to have around in the encampment and his wife, Nicola, well, a trained pharmacist was a handy thing to have around in the event of— And the kids, they could gather— O'Yee said desperately, 'I don't know what you're talking about!'

'The killing! You enjoy the killing, like me! The trophy's yours—the head!' The archer, leaning down further over Shen's body for support, said in a pleading voice, 'For the love of God, man, I'm wounded. For the love of God, do the right thing and finish me off—'

O'Yee said, *'No!'*

'You're a hunter! Do what's right!'

'No!' O'Yee said, 'I'm a backwoods—I'm a goddamned *cop!'* He tried to think, to hear the typhoon outside, but it was all gone, 'I'm a—'

Shen's gun was within his reach. It was caught by the hammer in his waistband, that was all. Just that. One tiny thing. The hammer on the Police Positive had come back a little and then caught around Shen's waistband and that was the only thing holding it. The archer could see the trigger guard free and the six inch barrel making a line parallel with the waistband where he had tried to wrench it out and it had become caught. The archer, coughing, said, 'It's people like you and me, we're the only ones left who understand what real life is. All these poncing little computer men and their little flashing boxes and their punch hole cards and their laws and rules—we're the only ones who know that it's all about killing your enemies and your game and—'

194

O'Yee felt his eyes going. They were losing focus. He saw the man's hand moving, but he couldn't make out where it was going. The blood was flowing freely down the side of his face and O'Yee thought, 'I've been hurt. Something's happened and I've been hurt.' He saw the archer's hand going towards something and he ordered him with sudden alarm, 'Don't move! You're under arrest! Just don't move!' O'Yee said warningly, 'You're lying to me. I know you're lying to me. It isn't true. I'm not a—I'm a—' He thought he saw something on the ground near the archer's hand and he thought, 'Shen. It's Shen...' His head was bursting. He shouted at the archer, 'Don't move! Just don't—' He thought he heard someone accuse him of something, his wife, or Feiffer or— O'Yee shouted, 'I'm me! I'm entitled to be who I want to be! If I want to be goddamned Pin then I will be!' He couldn't think. He had the smell of water in his nose, of the rapids on the Colorado river – he thought, 'No, I've never even seen the Colorado river' – and then the— *He couldn't think who he was!* O'Yee said, 'I'm—'

The archer's hand got to the gun and freed the hammer. The weapon moved easily. He turned it slightly in his hand and against the backplate facing the cylinder he could see that at least three chambers were loaded. The archer said evenly, soothingly, 'Maybe you're right. Maybe you're—' The gun came out cleanly. The man facing him was wandering, raving, his eyes coming in and out of focus. The archer, a slow smile forming on his face, said quietly, 'You're right, man, you be just who you like.' The weapon's hammer came back under his thumb with the faintest of faint clicks. The archer, leaning back to get the shot in from a kneeling position upwards to the heart, said reassuringly, 'After all, nobody wants to live forever, do they?'

It was coming back. Shen. It was Shen. And the blood, the blood was... He was a hunter, just like ... and the blood was— O'Yee said vaguely, 'No, I'm a—' *After he had*

killed him he had cut his tongue out and taken it away for a trophy!
O'Yee said, 'No! I'm a—' What? What?

He saw the gun beginning to come up and he simply couldn't remember.

*

There seemed to be almost nothing left of the station except rubble. The entire front wall was down and Feiffer, sloshing through the debris and water in the street, putting the big gun quickly under his coat to keep it dry, made for it with Spencer and Auden only feet behind him.

*

Of course he had been afraid when Koh had been killed! Who the hell wouldn't have been afraid? And that goddamned huge, enormous, great Arkansas toothpick, that god-damned thing *hurt* when you shaved with it. By God, if the truth be told, it bloody *hurt!*

What fur-bearing animals? You couldn't trap fur-bearing animals for fur because there were so few fur-bearing animals left that they were all protected and put safe in zoos so people like him could go and look at them. Like whales. You couldn't go off whaling anymore because there just weren't any whales left. People like him. People like him... People like him – you couldn't just go around killing things because you liked it because there just weren't enough things left – and Pine Cone Pin – he had killed to – maybe he didn't even like killing—

He didn't. O'Yee remembered. Pine Cone Pin had gone out of his apartment with his hunting rifle to protect his family and he hadn't— O'Yee shouted at the top of his voice, 'I'm not Pine Cone bloody Pin! I'm a goddamned—' O'Yee shouted at the archer, 'I'm a goddamned—' He saw the gun coming up, the black muzzle going higher and

196

higher in the archer's grip and he thought, 'You lied to me, you're not hurt at all—' His mind was racing, skidding off the track. O'Yee said, 'No, what I am is—' O'Yee shrieked at each one of his advancing forty years and long nights awake listening to the heart in his chest that in all probability wasn't going to stop for at least the same number of years again, 'What I am is a goddamned civilized *man of peace!*' and to prove it, as Feiffer and Auden and Spencer, also men of peace and armed to the teeth, burst in, taking instinctive aim and dropping him like a stone in the centre of the floor, O'Yee shot the archer cleanly and accurately twice, without malice, through the kneecaps.

17

So long as the new moon returns in heaven a bent, beautiful bow...

4.27 a.m. That night there was no moon and the last human soul in Fade Street after the typhoon and the clean-up squads had both completed their work was a solitary man walking his dog.

In the darkness he went the full length of the street only once, then, the dog whimpering a little for a pat, he leant down, stroked it on the muzzle and, his mind already on new schemes for the prosperity of his future, The Ex-Umbrella Man, having found no broken umbrellas for repair or resale, without real regret, went quickly and decisively on his way.